Junior Great Books

BOOK TWO

Junior Great Books®

Chicago, Illinois

ISBN 978-1-939014-76-4

2 4 6 8 9 7 5 3 1

Printed in the United States of America

Published and distributed by

THE GREAT BOOKS FOUNDATION

A nonprofit educational organization

35 East Wacker Drive, Suite 400

Chicago, IL 60601

www.greatbooks.org

CONTENTS

Integrity

Perspective

INTRODUCTION

Welcome to Book Two of Junior Great Books! Here are some reminders about what to expect as you use **Shared Inquiry**™—a way of reading and discussing great stories to explore what they mean.

How Shared Inquiry Works

You will begin by reading along as the story is read aloud. The group then shares questions about the story. Some questions will be answered right away, while others will be saved for the discussion or other activities.

After sharing questions, everyone reads the story again. During the second reading, you will do activities that help you think more deeply about specific parts of the story.

You will then develop your ideas about the story even more in **Shared Inquiry discussion**.

What Shared Inquiry Discussion Looks Like

Your teacher will start the discussion with an **interpretive question**—a question that has more than one good answer that can be supported with evidence from the story. In Shared Inquiry discussion, the goal is not to find the "right answer," but to work together to explore many different answers. Your teacher will ask more questions during the discussion to help everyone think deeply and explain their ideas.

In the discussion, you will give your answer to the interpretive question and back it up with evidence from the story. You will also tell your classmates what you think about their answers and ask them questions to learn more about their ideas.

Depending on the ideas you hear, you may add to or change your original answer to the question. When the discussion is over, people will have different answers to the interpretive question, but everyone will have evidence for those answers and will understand the story better.

Sometimes the class may work on projects after discussion that are related to the story, like writing, making art, or doing research.

You may find that even after the class has finished working on a story, you are still thinking about it. The characters and events in a story may help you think about your own life and the world around you in new ways, or they might bring up a subject you are interested in.

Every time you practice Shared Inquiry activities like asking questions, rereading, and discussing stories, you become a stronger reader and thinker.

Dos and Don'ts in Discussion

DO

Let other people talk, and listen to what they say.

DON'T

Talk while other people are talking.

DO

Share your ideas about the story. You may have an idea no one else has thought of.

DON'T

Be afraid to say what you're thinking about the story.

DO

Be polite when you disagree with someone.

DON'T

Get angry when someone disagrees with you.

DO

Pay attention to the person who is talking.

DON'T

Do things that make it hard for people to pay attention.

Shared Inquiry Discussion Guidelines

Following these guidelines in Shared Inquiry discussion will help everyone share ideas about the story and learn from one another.

1. Listen to or read the story twice before the discussion.

2. Discuss only the story that everyone has read.

3. Support your ideas with evidence from the story.

4. Listen to other people's ideas. You may agree or disagree with someone's answer, or ask a question about it.

5. Expect the teacher to only ask questions.

Asking Follow-Up Questions

In Junior Great Books, the teacher isn't the only person who can ask questions. *You* can also ask questions if a classmate says something you want to know more about or understand better. These kinds of questions are called **follow-up questions**.

To ask good follow-up questions, you need to really **listen to what your classmates are saying**. When you listen closely, you will hear details that you may want to hear more about. On the next page are some examples of questions you might ask during a discussion or other Junior Great Books activities.

Remember:

- **You can also agree and disagree with your classmates**. Speak directly to them instead of only talking to the teacher, and explain why you agree or disagree.
- **A follow-up question is a compliment**. When you ask a follow-up question, you show that you are listening to and thinking about what others are saying. When someone asks you a question, they are interested in your ideas.

Things you might hear from your classmates:	Follow-up questions you might ask:
Words or phrases that you don't quite understand	"What do you mean?" "Can you say that again?"
An idea you want to know more about	"Can you say more about that?" "Why do you think that?"
An idea that needs to be backed up with evidence from the story	"What part of the story made you think that?" "Where does that happen in the story?"

Theme Introduction

Strength

In this section of the book, you will read about characters who show strength in different ways. Thinking about these stories, and about your own experiences, will give you new ideas about what it means to be strong.

Important Questions to Think About

Before starting this section, think about your own experiences with strength:

- Can you think of a time when you were strong, or when you struggled to be strong?
- Is there someone in your life that you admire for their strength?

Once you have thought about your own experiences with strength, think about this **theme question** and write down your answers or share them aloud:

What does it mean to be strong?

After reading each story in this section, ask yourself the theme question again. You may have some new ideas you want to add.

My mother sang as she combed my hair.

TUESDAY OF THE OTHER JUNE

Norma Fox Mazer

"Be good, be good, be good, be good, my Junie," my mother sang as she combed my hair—a song, a story, a croon, a plea. "It's just you and me, two women alone in the world, June darling of my heart. We have enough troubles getting by, we surely don't need a single one more, so you keep your sweet self out of fighting and all that bad stuff. People can be little hearted, but turn the other cheek, smile at the world, and the world'll surely smile back."

We stood in front of the mirror as she combed my hair, combed and brushed and smoothed. Her head came just above mine; she said when I grew another inch she'd stand on a stool to brush my hair. "I'm not giving up this pleasure!" And she laughed her long honey laugh.

My mother was April, my grandmother had been May, I was June. "And someday," said my mother, "you'll have a daughter of your own. What will you name her?"

"January!" I'd yell when I was little. "February! No, November!" My mother laughed her honey laugh. She had little emerald eyes that warmed me like the sun.

Every day when I went to school, she went to work. "Sometimes I stop what I'm doing," she said, "lay down my tools, and stop everything, because all I can think about is you. Wondering what you're doing and if you need me. Now, Junie, if anyone ever bothers you—"

"—I walk away, run away, come on home as fast as my feet will take me," I recited.

"Yes. You come to me. You just bring me your trouble, because I'm here on this earth to love you and take care of you."

I was safe with her. Still, sometimes I woke up at night and heard footsteps slowly creeping up the stairs. It wasn't my mother—she was asleep in the bed across the room—so it was robbers, thieves, and murderers, creeping slowly . . . slowly . . . slowly toward my bed.

I stuffed my hand into my mouth. If I screamed and woke her, she'd be tired at work tomorrow. The robbers and thieves filled the warm darkness and slipped across the floor more quietly than cats. Rigid under the covers, I stared at the shifting dark and bit my knuckles and never knew when I fell asleep again.

In the morning we sang in the kitchen. "Bill Grogan's GOAT! Was feelin' FINE! Ate three red shirts, right off the LINE!" I made sandwiches for our lunches, she made pancakes for breakfast, but all she ate was one pancake and a cup of coffee. "Gotta fly, can't be late."

I wanted to be rich and take care of her. She worked too hard; her pretty hair had gray in it that she joked about. "Someday," I said, "I'll buy you a real house, and you'll never work in a pot factory again."

"Such delicious plans," she said. She checked the windows to see if they were locked. "Do you have your key?"

I lifted it from the chain around my neck.

"And you'll come right home from school and—"

"—I won't light fires or let strangers into the house, and I won't tell anyone on the phone that I'm here alone," I finished for her.

"I know, I'm just your old worrywart mother." She kissed me twice, once on each cheek. "But you are my June, my only June, the only June."

She was wrong; there was another June. I met her when we stood next to each other at the edge of the pool the first day of swimming class in the community center.

"What's your name?" She had a deep growly voice.

"June. What's yours?"

She stared at me. "June."

"We have the same name."

"No we don't. June is *my* name, and I don't give you permission to use it. Your name is Fish Eyes." She pinched me hard. "Got it, Fish Eyes?"

The next Tuesday, the Other June again stood next to me at the edge of the pool. "What's your name?"

"June."

"Wrong. Your—name—is—Fish—Eyes."

"June."

"Fish Eyes, you are really stupid." She shoved me into the pool.

The swimming teacher looked up, frowning, from her chart. "No one in the water yet."

Later, in the locker room, I dressed quickly and wrapped my wet suit in the towel. The Other June pulled on her jeans. "You guys see that bathing suit Fish Eyes was wearing? Her mother found it in a trash can."

"She did not!"

The Other June grabbed my fingers and twisted. "Where'd she find your bathing suit?"

"She bought it; let me go."

"Poor little stupid Fish Eyes is crying. Oh, boo hoo hoo, poor little Fish Eyes."

After that, everyone called me Fish Eyes. And every Tuesday, wherever I was, there was also the Other June—at the edge of the pool, in the pool, in the locker room. In the water, she swam alongside me, blowing and huffing, knocking into me. In the locker room, she stepped on my feet, pinched my arms, hid my blouse, and knotted my braids together. She had large square teeth; she was shorter than I was, but heavier, with bigger bones and square hands. If I met her outside on the street, carrying her bathing suit and towel, she'd walk toward me, smiling a square, friendly smile. "Oh well, if it isn't Fish Eyes." Then she'd punch me, *blam*! Her whole solid weight hitting me.

I didn't know what to do about her. She was training me like a dog. After a few weeks of this, she only had to look at me, only had to growl, "I'm going to get you, Fish Eyes," for my heart to slink like a whipped dog down into my stomach. My arms were covered with bruises. When my mother noticed, I made up a story about tripping on the sidewalk.

My weeks were no longer Tuesday, Wednesday, Thursday, and so on. Tuesday was Awfulday. Wednesday was Badday. (The Tuesday bad feelings were still there.) Thursday was Betterday and Friday was Safeday. Saturday was Goodday, but Sunday was Toosoonday, and Monday—Monday was nothing but the day before Awfulday.

I tried to slow down time. Especially on the weekends, I stayed close by my mother, doing everything with her, shopping, cooking, cleaning, going to the laundromat. "Aw, sweetie, go play with your friends."

"No, I'd rather be with you." I wouldn't look at the clock or listen to the radio (they were always telling you the date and the time). I did special magic things to keep the day from going away, rapping my knuckles six times on the bathroom door six times a day and never, ever touching the chipped place on my bureau. But always I woke up to the day before Tuesday, and always, no matter how many times

I circled the worn spot in the living-room rug or counted twenty-five cracks in the ceiling, Monday disappeared and once again it was Tuesday.

The Other June got bored with calling me Fish Eyes. Buffalo Brain came next, but as soon as everyone knew that, she renamed me Turkey Nose.

Now at night it wasn't robbers creeping up the stairs, but the Other June, coming to torment me. When I finally fell asleep, I dreamed of kicking her, punching, biting, pinching. In the morning, I remembered my dreams and felt brave and strong. And then I remembered all the things my mother had taught me and told me.

Be good, be good, be good, it's just us two women alone in the world . . . Oh, but if it weren't, if my father wasn't long gone, if we'd had someone else to fall back on, if my mother's mother and daddy weren't dead all these years, if my father's daddy wanted to know us instead of being glad to forget us—oh, then I would have punched the Other June with a frisky heart; I would have grabbed her arm at poolside and bitten her like the dog she had made of me.

One night, when my mother came home from work, she said, "Junie, listen to this. We're moving!"

Alaska, I thought. Florida. Arizona. Someplace far away and wonderful, someplace without the Other June.

"Wait till you hear this deal. We are going to be caretakers, troubleshooters for an eight-family apartment building. Fifty-six Blue Hill Street. Not janitors, we don't do any of the heavy work. April and June, Troubleshooters, Incorporated. If a tenant has a complaint or a problem, she comes to us, and we either take care of it or call the janitor for service. And for that little bit of work, we get to live rent free!" She swept me around in a dance. "Okay? You like it? I do!"

So. Not anywhere else, really. All the same, maybe too far to go to swimming class? "Can we move right away? Today?"

"Gimme a break, sweetie. We've got to pack, do a thousand things. I've got to line up someone with a truck to help us. Six weeks, Saturday the fifteenth." She circled it on the calendar. It was the Saturday after the last day of swimming class.

Soon, we had boxes lying everywhere, filled with clothes and towels and glasses wrapped in newspaper. Bit by bit, we cleared the rooms, leaving only what we needed right now. The dining-room table staggered on a bunched-up rug, our bureaus inched toward the front door like patient cows. On the calendar in the kitchen, my mother marked off the days until we moved, but the only days I thought about were Tuesdays—Awfuldays. Nothing else was real except the too-fast passing of time, moving toward each Tuesday . . . away from Tuesday . . . toward Tuesday. . . .

And it seemed to me that this would go on forever—that Tuesdays would come forever and I would be forever trapped by the side of the pool, the Other June whispering *Buffalo Brain Fish Eyes Turkey Nose* into my ear, while she ground her elbow into my side and smiled her square smile at the swimming teacher.

And then it ended. It was the last day of swimming class. The last Tuesday. We had all passed our tests and, as if in celebration, the Other June only pinched me twice. "And now," our swimming teacher said, "all of you are ready for the advanced class, which starts in just one month. I have a sign-up slip here. Please put your name down before you leave." Everyone but me crowded around. I went to the locker room and pulled on my clothes as fast as possible. The Other June burst through the door just as I was leaving. "Goodbye," I yelled. "Good riddance to bad trash!" Before she could pinch me again, I ran past her and then ran all the way home, singing, "Goodbye . . . good-bye . . . goodbye, good riddance to bad trash!"

Later, my mother carefully untied the blue ribbon around my swimming class diploma. "Look at this! Well, isn't this wonderful! You are on your way, you might turn into an Olympic swimmer, you never know what life will bring."

"I don't want to take more lessons."

"Oh, sweetie, it's great to be a good swimmer." But then, looking into my face, she said, "No, no, no, don't worry; you don't have to."

The next morning, I woke up hungry for the first time in weeks. No more swimming class. No more Baddays and Awfuldays. No more Tuesdays of the Other June. In the kitchen, I made hot cocoa to go with my mother's corn muffins. "It's Wednesday, Mom," I said, stirring the cocoa. "My favorite day."

"Since when?"

"Since this morning." I turned on the radio so I could hear the announcer tell the time, the temperature, and the day.

Thursday for breakfast I made cinnamon toast, Friday my mother made pancakes, and on Saturday, before we moved, we ate the last slices of bread and cleaned out the peanut butter jar.

"Some breakfast," Tilly said. "Hello, you must be June." She shook my hand. She was a friend of my mother's from work; she wore big hoop earrings, sandals, and a skirt as dazzling as a rainbow. She came in a truck with John to help us move our things.

John shouted cheerfully at me, "So you're moving." An enormous man with a face covered with little brown bumps. Was he afraid his voice wouldn't travel the distance from his mouth to my ear? "You looking at my moles?" he shouted, and he heaved our big green flowered chair down the stairs. "Don't worry, they don't bite. Ha, ha, ha!" Behind him came my mother and Tilly balancing a bureau between them, and behind them I carried a lamp and the round, flowered Mexican tray that was my mother's favorite. She had found it at a garage sale and said it was as close to foreign travel as we would ever get.

The night before, we had loaded our car, stuffing in bags and boxes until there was barely room for the two of us. But it was only when we were in the car, when we drove past Abdo's Grocery, where they always gave us credit, when I turned for a last look at our street—it was only then that I understood we were truly going to live somewhere else, in another apartment, in another place mysteriously called Blue Hill Street.

Tilly's truck followed our car.

"Oh, I'm so excited," my mother said. She laughed. "You'd think we were going across the country."

Our old car wheezed up a long, steep hill. Blue Hill Street. I looked from one side to the other, trying to see everything.

My mother drove over the crest of the hill. "And now—ta da!—our new home."

"Which house? Which one?" I looked out the window and what I saw was the Other June. She was sprawled on the stoop of a pink house, lounging back on her elbows, legs outspread, her jaws working on a wad of gum. I slid down into the seat, but it was too late. I was sure she had seen me.

My mother turned into a driveway next to a big white building with a tiny porch. She leaned on the steering wheel. "See that window there, that's our living-room window . . . and that one over there, that's your bedroom. . . ."

We went into the house, down a dim, cool hall. In our new apartment, the wooden floors clicked under our shoes, and my mother showed me everything. Her voice echoed in the empty rooms. I followed her around in a daze. Had I imagined seeing the Other June? Maybe I'd seen another girl who looked like her. A double. That could happen.

"Ho yo, where do you want this chair?" John appeared in the doorway. We brought in boxes and bags and beds and stopped only to eat pizza and drink orange juice from the carton.

"June's so quiet; do you think she'll adjust all right?" I heard Tilly say to my mother.

"Oh, definitely. She'll make a wonderful adjustment. She's just getting used to things."

But I thought that if the Other June lived on the same street as I did, I would never get used to things.

That night I slept in my own bed, with my own pillow and blanket, but with floors that creaked in strange voices and walls with cracks I didn't recognize. I didn't feel either happy or unhappy. It was as if I were waiting for something.

Monday, when the principal of Blue Hill Street School left me in Mr. Morrisey's classroom, I knew what I'd been waiting for. In that room full of strange kids, there was one person I knew. She smiled her square smile, raised her hand, and said, "She can sit next to me, Mr. Morrisey."

"Very nice of you, June M. Okay, June T, take your seat. I'll try not to get you two Junes mixed up."

I sat down next to her. She pinched my arm. "Good riddance to bad trash," she mocked.

I was back in the Tuesday swimming class only now it was worse, because every day would be

Awfulday. The pinching had already started. Soon, I knew, on the playground and in the halls, kids would pass me, grinning. "Hiya, Fish Eyes."

The Other June followed me around during recess that day, droning in my ear, "You are my slave. You must do everything I say. I am your master. Say it, say, 'Yes, master, you are my master.'"

I pressed my lips together, clapped my hands over my ears, but without hope. Wasn't it only a matter of time before I said the hateful words?

"How was school?" my mother said that night.

"Okay."

She put a pile of towels in a bureau drawer. "Try not to be sad about missing your old friends, sweetie. There'll be new ones."

The next morning, the Other June was waiting for me when I left the house. "Did your mother get you that blouse in the garbage dump?" She butted me, shoving me against a tree. "Don't you speak anymore, Fish Eyes?" Grabbing my chin in her hands, she pried open my mouth. "Oh, ha ha, I thought you lost your tongue."

We went on to school. I sank down into my seat, my head on my arms. "June T, are you all right?" Mr. Morrisey asked. I nodded. My head was almost too heavy to lift.

The Other June went to the pencil sharpener. Round and round she whirled the handle. Walking back, looking at me, she held the three sharp pencils like three little knives.

Someone knocked on the door. Mr. Morrisey went out into the hall. Paper planes burst into the air, flying from desk to desk. Someone turned on a transistor radio. And the Other June, coming closer, smiled and licked her lips like a cat sleepily preparing to gulp down a mouse.

I remembered my dream of kicking her, punching, biting her like a dog.

Then my mother spoke quickly in my ear: *Turn the other cheek, my Junie, smile at the world and the world'll surely smile back.*

But I had turned the other cheek, and it was slapped. I had smiled, and the world hadn't smiled back. I couldn't run home as fast as my feet would take me; I had to stay in school—and in school there was the Other June. Every morning, there would be the Other June, and every afternoon, and every day, all day, there would be the Other June.

She frisked down the aisle, stabbing the pencils in the air toward me. A boy stood up on his desk and bowed. "My fans," he said, "I greet you." My arm twitched and throbbed, as if the Other June's pencils had already poked through the skin. She came closer, smiling her Tuesday smile.

"No," I whispered, "*no.*" The word took wings and flew me to my feet, in front of the Other June. "*Noooooo.*" It flew out of my mouth into her surprised face.

The boy on the desk turned toward us. "You said something, my devoted fans?"

"No," I said to the Other June. "Oh, no! No. No. No. No more." I pushed away the hand that held the pencils.

The Other June's eyes opened, popped wide like the eyes of somebody in a cartoon. It made me laugh. The boy on the desk laughed, and then the other kids were laughing, too.

"No," I said again, because it felt so good to say it. "No, no, no, no." I leaned toward the Other June, put my finger against her chest. Her cheeks turned red, she squawked something—it sounded like "Eeeraaghyou!"—and she stepped back. She stepped away from me.

The door banged, the airplanes disappeared, and Mr. Morrisey walked to his desk. "Okay. Okay. Let's get back to work. Kevin Clark, how about it?" Kevin jumped off the desk, and Mr. Morrisey picked up a piece of chalk. "All right, class—" He stopped and looked at me and the Other June. "You two Junes, what's going on there?"

I tried it again. My finger against her chest. Then the words. "No—more." And she stepped back another step. I sat down at my desk.

"June M," Mr. Morrisey said.

She turned around, staring at him with that big-eyed cartoon look. After a moment she sat down at her desk with a loud slapping sound.

Even Mr. Morrisey laughed.

And sitting at my desk, twirling my braids, I knew this was the last Tuesday of the Other June.

Grandpa had followed the buffalo.

Doesn't Fall Off His Horse

Virginia A. Stroud

Saygee's great-grandfather was a slender man, and not very tall, but his hands and face showed his age, strength, and wisdom.

He sat on the edge of his bed facing the window, watching the patterns of light from the setting sun play on the fenced yard. He watched the birds, the clouds, and a spider that was building its web. He watched the memories in his head.

"Grandpa," Saygee called softly. "Grandpa!"

This time he heard her. Slowly he turned his entire body around to face the doorway of his bedroom, his wire-framed glasses making his eyes look much larger than they really were.

A smile appeared across his face as he recognized his youngest great-granddaughter, and he raised his arm to greet Saygee. “Good to see you,” he said. “Sit, sit.” He slapped the bed beside him.

There were no exchanges of polite conversation with Grandpa, no “How are you, how have you been?” To him that was obvious: You were all right; you were with him.

They sat in silence as Saygee looked outdoors with him. When he was ready to talk, he would let her know.

In Saygee's household, children learned to watch for direction, not to ask questions; for the answers were available by watching. So she sat and watched with him for a bit, not wanting to interrupt his study of the earth. When his thoughts were finished, he patted her hand and smiled, giving her permission to speak.

Saygee wanted to ask Grandpa for a story, but which one? He was like a living book; nearly a hundred years had passed under his footsteps during his walk upon the earth. He had followed the buffalo, he had roamed the open plains with tepee and lodge poles, he'd seen the non-Indian wagons come to Indian Territory and watched from a hilltop as the settlers staked out the land. He saw one of the first locomotives cut across the prairie, then an automobile and an airplane; he had received the citizenship given to the Native American people. Many changes had come for his people, the Kiowas, in those years, and for him as well.

The little man's voice suddenly pierced the silence. "Doesn't Fall Off His Horse."

"Who doesn't fall off his horse, Grandpa?" Saygee asked.

"Me." He smiled with pride. "That's my Indian name, 'Doesn't Fall Off His Horse.' " He began to unfasten the top button of his red flannel shirt.

"You see?" He leaned forward. "See my neck—here, this side," and he motioned with the flat side of his left hand from his chin to his earlobe. "The bullet took half my neck. I thought I was a goner. . . . But Doesn't Fall Off His Horse is still here, walking this good road," he added with a wink and a nod to Saygee.

Grandpa cleared his throat and reached for a cigarette off his nightstand. Saygee wrinkled her nose but remained quiet, listening. "Over there," he said, pointing with his chin and lower lip. "Over there in that trunk is a white sheet. Bring it and its contents to me."

Saygee got up and headed toward the old leather-bound stagecoach trunk. Kneeling, she unfastened the wooden bar straps and opened the lid.

On top, just as Grandpa had said, was a long object wrapped in a white sheet. Grandpa reached out, impatient for her to lay the treasure in his lap. With one slow turn and another, he folded back the sheet. "There," he said, smiling as he exposed its contents.

"A quiver," Saygee said.

"Yes." He stroked the quiver gently. "Do you see the hide? It's leopard skin from India, very rare. I had to do a lot of trading with the white traders to get this hide. I exchanged one bow and two buffalo robes. It's my old friend. I took it everywhere with me—though there was a time when it didn't help me make a coup."

"What's a coup, Grandpa?" Saygee asked.

“Coup is like a game of tag—a very serious and dangerous game that we played to embarrass and show dishonor to the enemy tribes. A warrior could count coup in several ways. He could enter the enemy’s village, run and touch a tepee with his bare hand, and leave without being caught; or in battle he might hit his enemy with an object in his hand—a bow, a lance, or a coup stick. The purpose was not to kill your enemy, but to shame him for being off guard. A warrior counting coup could even steal horses from the enemy tribe.”

"Steal horses, Grandpa?" Saygee interrupted, not believing her good grandpa would ever steal.

He smiled at her. "I know what you're thinking: It isn't right to steal. We would not have dreamed of taking a friend's possessions. But we sometimes took ponies from our enemies so they would be short of horses and could not raid our villages. This would also give our tribe fresh horses for our survival.

"Counting coup," Grandpa continued, "gave honor to the individual warrior and to the entire tribe. The warrior who made a coup was looked upon as a hero, and sometimes his warrior name would be earned.

"My friends and I would often hear the elder warriors speak of the coups they had made. We would sit, green with envy, listening spellbound to their adventures."

His eyes gazed out into the twilight sky. Then he began to speak again.

◆ ◆ ◆

"I don't know what year it was, because we didn't have calendars. It was a good time, though.

"My friends and brothers were alive then, and active. We'd play games with bows and arrows, perfecting our skills by hunting rabbits or even butterflies. We raced our ponies bareback in open fields, or watched the women make shields and tan the soft hides.

"To this day I have no idea which one of us began talking about stealing ponies from the Comanches camped south of us. But for days all we talked about were the ponies and the raid.

"I was sleeping on my pallet. Camp was silent. Then I heard a familiar voice outside my father's tepee whisper, 'Tonight, now, come.' It was my friend Tali, our ringleader.

"Getting out of our tepee without waking my parents would be much harder than raiding the Comanche ponies, I thought. I sat up, almost afraid to breathe. Mother was a light sleeper, and at any break in the breathing patterns of her children, she would rise quickly.

"I made my breath deep and even, so as not to cause alarm. Then I stood with my bow and leopard skin quiver in one hand, plotting my steps to the tepee flap across from me. I had to step around four bodies and get past the dogs to meet my friends. Part of me said, 'Just go'; the other part said, 'Lie back down!' One foot and then another and I was outside the tepee flap under open skies.

" 'Come on, hurry!' whispered Tali, waving me over to join him and three others by the side of a tree. My steps were light as I ran in a crouched position, sweat beading over my lip and forehead.

"We were waiting for one more friend, but he had not yet appeared from his tepee. I felt a tap on my shoulder from behind and Tali beckoned me to follow. 'We can't wait any longer; it will be sunrise soon,' he said. 'As it is, we are going to have to ride hard to get to the Comanche camp without being seen!'

"Our ponies were hobbled in an area beside the stream. There was no moon, which made our escape easier. As we hid under the bellies of our ponies, we could see the watchers of the camp walking around the village. We threw blankets over the horses' heads so they wouldn't make any noise or rear up on us as we untied their hobbles and led them away from camp.

"A safe distance later we jumped on the ponies' backs, and away we rode toward the Comanche camp.

"My heart was pounding as we rode. I think the ponies sensed we were up to something; they were both fast and alert. Our goal was to enter the enemy

camp, take their horses, and bring them back to our camp—all without being seen.

"The Oklahoma prairies were flat and full of prairie dog holes. The horses could step into the holes and break their legs, but we ran them as hard as we could all the same. When you're young, you sometimes do things that are not so smart. It's when you're older that you realize you should have taken precautions.

"As we rode farther south, the air carried the smell of smoke, and we knew we were close to the Comanche camp. Scrub oak bushes and cottonwood trees clustered by the stream.

“ ‘We’ll tie the ponies over there,’ said Tali, pointing to the scrub oak. ‘Reed will stay with our horses so they don’t run off before we need them.’

“From here on we would approach on our stomachs, inching our way to the Comanche ponies tied across the campgrounds. ‘Check the wind direction. Look for the camp watchers; nobody gives us away. If you get scared, stay put; don’t stand or run.’ These were our orders from Tali.

"I could still hear my heart pounding in my ears and quickly asked the Great Spirit to guide me; to help me gather my swiftness and intuition, and make my eyesight sharp and sense of smell keen as an animal's. 'Be as a deer,' I told myself.

"The Comanche ponies stirred as we approached. The watchers were nowhere in sight. We had to unhobble the horses, throw ropes around their necks, if time permitted, and escape. No time to use blankets to cover the eyes of the enemies' horses, so we grabbed their noses to keep them from making noises that would wake the village.

"I was hiding between the legs and bellies of the horses, working quickly to cut the hobbles. One kicked another in the flank; a fight was about to break out among them. I could see the whites of their eyes, and their ears were lying flat against their heads.

" 'Let's go!' I heard. I grabbed ropes that were around two of the horses' necks and mounted one of the Comanche ponies; my friends did the same. I herded the loose animals in front of me as we broke for open land.

"A man's deep voice called from behind our backs. We'd been spotted, and watchers were ready for us.

"A Comanche warrior jumped out from behind the scrub oak, startling my horse. The pony darted right, then left and around the man as he waved his raised arms above his head, warning me to stop. I hung tightly to the lead ropes of the two horses that followed and continued to drive the loose ponies ahead of me.

" 'Ride hard. They are coming!' Reed shouted, pulling alongside us at full speed with our Kiowa ponies. I turned to see mounted Comanche warriors following close behind with rifles.

"Rifle fire zinged past my head, and I flattened myself against my horse's neck as its hooves pounded the prairie. I checked again behind me, and I could see the Comanche warriors slowing down. As I sat upright on my horse, one more round of gunfire pierced the open skies.

"I felt warm liquid on my shoulder and face. Rain, I thought, and checked the starlit night sky. Then I sensed a burning sensation on my neck as my body recognized the wound.

"For a while everything seemed to move in slow motion and the pounding hooves were silent. Still clutching the two horses' ropes, I fell forward on my pony's neck, holding my arms and legs tight around its body. I had a sensation that someone was sitting behind me on the horse, sort of holding me in place, not letting me fall, as I bounced around like a rag doll.

" 'Camp!' shouted Tali. 'Hold on!' The sun was breaking through the darkness. It wasn't over the horizon yet, but movement was visible in the camp. It was good to see the familiar clothes of my people.

"The women sang their high-pitched loo-loos of praise as they witnessed our approach. My friends whooped and yelled to celebrate our successful coup, awakening the rest of the village. My pony came to an abrupt halt, and I was carried off its back.

"Later I was told that my hands had to be pried from the ropes attached to the ponies that I'd pulled across the prairie. I had lost much blood, and half my neck was ripped loose from the Comanche bullet.

"The medicine woman housed me within the tepee walls of the medicine lodge. Her assistants cut a prickly pear leaf, split it, and placed it on my neck. No one thought I was going to live, but within four sunsets I was drinking water from a reed straw.

"When I was able to sit up on my own, four elders entered the medicine lodge together with family members and my friends from the raid.

" 'What you boys did showed bad judgment,' said one of the elders.

" 'You could have put this entire camp in danger with your foolishness,' said another. 'We are not at war with this enemy. Stealing horses is a war deed only!'

" 'No one is permitted to make decisions on his own without the counsel of the tribal leaders,' the third told me.

" 'Also, what you did was very brave,' said the fourth elder. 'The people here needed fresh horses. For that you did well. You have been shot. That is enough punishment for you. Even though you were

badly wounded, you didn't let go of your stolen horses or fall from your horse. You have made your first coup and have earned your warrior name. From now on you will be called "Doesn't Fall Off His Horse.'" Then the elders left the medicine lodge.

"It took a long time to recover from my wounds, and that was the last time my friends and I raided alone."

◆ ◆ ◆

Grandpa looked down at his leopard skin quiver and began to wrap the white sheet around it.

"I've never heard that story, Grandpa," Saygee said.

"Today you found me remembering my youth, when my eyes were clear and my walk had purpose." He reached for his pillow, propped it behind him, and slowly leaned back on his bed, looking out the window and cradling his quiver. Then he took another cigarette, lit it, and said, "That's all."

Saygee knew that she was being dismissed. Her visit was over.

"Want your light on, Grandpa?" she asked. He didn't take his eyes away from the window, nor did he answer her. She could see that he was with his memories again; he was with Doesn't Fall Off His Horse.

How he plays, our Mr. O!

The Cello of Mr. O

Jane Cutler

Here we are, surrounded and under attack.

My father and most of the other fathers, the older brothers—even some of the grandfathers—have gone to fight. So we stay, children and women, the old and the sick, managing as best we can.

I am afraid almost all the time.

At night, from my window, I can see the white trails of tracer fire and the orange flash of mortars in the sky. I pretend I am watching shooting stars and meteors.

The streets of our city are littered with bricks, dust, and broken glass. We have no heating oil. Last winter, we slept in our clothes in the kitchen, next to a sheet-metal stove Papa put together before he left.

We used up all our wood. If something doesn't change by the time winter comes again, we will have to burn furniture and books to keep warm.

Food is scarce, of course. And water. We collect rainwater in bowls and buckets. And we go to distribution centers and bring water home.

Some people carry their heavy containers of water in shopping carts, some in wheelbarrows. In winter, many of us use sleds. Last week, Mama and I saw a woman hauling water in a wheelchair.

Each Wednesday at four, the relief truck comes to a street right outside our square. We wait in line to receive soap, cooking oil, canned fish, flour.

Nothing is as it was: shops, cars, and apartments have been destroyed. Schools are closed, the electricity is usually out, and there is no gas at all. Even the telephones don't work.

Many people have left.

Some, like Mama's friend Marya, stay because they have no place else to go. And some, like my mother, have decided to stay—no matter what.

Mama can't stand the idea of Papa coming back to nothing. She wants us to be here.

Mama sighs. "This is not the first time in history that such a thing has happened," she tells me.

It may not be the first time it has happened. But it is the first time it has happened to me.

I am angry almost all the time.

My friends and I stay close to home, usually inside our large apartment building, sitting under the stairs. We pass the time playing cards and word games. Reading books. Drawing. Talking. We imagine what we would have if we could eat whatever we wanted.

Sometimes we can't sit still a minute longer, and we run through the halls, laughing and making noise.

Then Mr. O flings open his door. "Quiet, you kids!" he shouts. As if kids were a bad thing.

When the relief truck comes at four o'clock on Wednesdays, everyone goes into the street. It feels like a party, being outside with so many other people for a change.

Even Mr. O stands in line.

But he doesn't chat. He just waits, looking away from the rest of us.

"A thinker," my mother says quietly, nodding in his direction.

"A thinker," her friend Marya says, but in a mocking tone.

Marya doesn't agree with my mother. Neither do I. Mr. O isn't thinking. He is just being unfriendly.

We children don't like Mr. O. Whenever one of us can find a paper bag, we blow it up with air and then pop it right outside his apartment door. It sounds just like a shell exploding!

We laugh and run, imagining his fear.

When he is not waiting in line for supplies with the rest of us, Mr. O plays his cello.

It is a fine cello, one of the best. My father, who loves music, too—who plays tender songs and lively tunes on the harmonica—told me this about the cello of Mr. O.

"The front and the back of that excellent cello were carved out of German fiddleback maple and hand-rubbed with a special polish made in France," said my father.

"The neck of the cello was made of mahogany from Honduras, and the fingerboard of ebony, probably from Ceylon," he said.

"As for the bow," my father continued, "it was carved out of a soft wood that grows in Brazil. The ivory on its tip came from Africa."

"People all over the world had to cooperate to make the cello of Mr. O," my father said.

My father told me about Mr. O, too. "When he was young, he traveled around the world, playing his cello in great halls for hundreds of people who cheered when he finished, and threw flowers."

If my father knew about the paper bags, he would be angry.

But Papa is far away, fighting somewhere in the mountains. He has taken his harmonica and all his warm clothes with him, and we have no idea when we will see him again.

It is four o'clock in the afternoon, a dull fall Wednesday. My friend Elena and I are playing jacks under the stairs. We hear the supply truck roar up. But we are lazy, and for once, we don't rush outside to wait with the others.

We hear the footsteps of people leaving their apartments, leaving the building.

We hear the murmur of talk and laughter.

Then we hear the rocket hit.

The truck is destroyed. Some people we know are badly hurt.

Now, even though we clear away the rubble and smooth over the ground, supplies will not be brought here. We are too easy a target, they tell us. Now we will have to walk for miles to get anything, and nothing will happen to make even one day a week better than the others.

But on the first Wednesday after the rocket, at exactly four o'clock, Mr. O appears, all dressed up, carrying his cello, carrying a chair.

He marches out into the middle of the square, where everyone can see him.

He sets up his chair.

He takes out his cello.

He tightens his horsehair bow and rubs it with rosin.

Then he takes a deep breath.

He plays.

"The music of Bach," Mama tells me, her face shining, as we listen to the complicated music, the powerful and reassuring notes.

How he plays, our Mr. O! As if he were on the stage of a grand, warm hall, playing for people who will throw flowers. As if he were not alone in the center of a deserted square in a besieged city, where even a relief truck will no longer come.

"They will kill him!" Marya cries fearfully.

"They would not bother to kill an old man playing a cello," Mama says.

I am not so sure.

Because the music of the cello makes us feel less angry. And the courage of the cellist makes us less afraid.

If they guess, it could be reason enough for them to want to stop the music, which feeds us as truly as the supplies brought by the truck did.

Mr. O does not play only on Wednesdays. Every day at four o'clock, he and his cello appear.

One day, after he has started playing, Mr. O gets a cramp in his leg. He leans the cello against his chair and hobbles about, shaking his leg.

We hear a fusillade of exploding shells.

We see clouds of black smoke.

Finally, when the smoke clears, we see that the cellist is unharmed. But all that remains of the cello is splintered wood and tangled strings.

What will feed us now? I wonder.

It is the very next day that I find the brown paper bag. It is a small one, and crumpled. I smooth it out as best I can. Then I put it under Papa's heavy dictionary and leave it there all night.

In the morning, I choose the best crayons I have from the cigar box where I keep them. Most of them are now just stubs of crayons. Still, I have many different colors left.

Carefully, on the crinkly paper bag, I draw. I draw a picture of Mr. O in his dark suit sitting on a chair, playing a cello. Then I draw bright flowers falling all around him.

When I finish, I take the picture and tiptoe up to Mr. O's apartment. I press my ear against the door and listen. Silence. Carefully, quietly, I slip the picture underneath the door. And then I run.

To everyone's surprise, promptly at four o'clock that afternoon, out of the building comes Mr. O, carrying a chair.

He sees me at my window, and he bows to me and smiles.

Then, from the pocket of his coat, he draws a small, shiny object. A harmonica!

From then on, for one hour every single day, Mr. O sits in the square and plays his harmonica.

The melodies sound sad and sweet and small, and very different from the grand songs Mr. O played on his cello.

"It is Bach, nevertheless," Mama says.

The music makes us feel happy.

And the courage of the harmonica player makes us less afraid.

Theme Introduction

Integrity

In this section of the book, you will read about characters who do what they think is right, or learn how to behave in a good and honest way. Thinking about these stories, and about your own experiences, will give you new ideas about what it means to have integrity.

Important Questions to Think About

Before starting this section, think about your own experiences with integrity:

- Can you remember a time when you did what you thought was right or honest even though it was difficult?
- Is there a person you know who shows great integrity? How do they show it?

Once you have thought about your own experiences with integrity, think about this **theme question** and write down your answers or share them aloud:

What does it mean to have integrity?

After reading each story in this section, ask yourself the theme question again. You may have some new ideas you want to add.

"I found your dog by the freeway."

THE NO-GUITAR BLUES

Gary Soto

The moment Fausto saw the group Los Lobos on *American Bandstand,* he knew exactly what he wanted to do with his life—play guitar. His eyes grew large with excitement as Los Lobos ground out a song while teenagers bounced off each other on the crowded dance floor.

He had watched *American Bandstand* for years and had heard Ray Camacho and the Teardrops at Romain Playground, but it had never occurred to him that he too might become a musician. That afternoon Fausto knew his mission in life: to play guitar in his own band, to sweat out his songs and prance around the stage, to make money and dress weird.

Fausto turned off the television set and walked outside, wondering how he could get enough money to buy a guitar. He couldn't ask his parents because they would just say, "Money doesn't grow on trees" or "What do you think we are, bankers?" And besides, they hated rock music. They were into the *conjunto* music of Lydia Mendoza, Flaco Jimenez, and Little Joe and La Familia. And, as Fausto recalled, the last album they bought was *The Chipmunks Sing Christmas Favorites.*

But what the heck, he'd give it a try. He returned inside and watched his mother make tortillas. He leaned against the kitchen counter, trying to work up the nerve to ask her for a guitar. Finally, he couldn't hold back any longer.

"Mom," he said, "I want a guitar for Christmas."

She looked up from rolling tortillas. "Honey, a guitar costs a lot of money."

"How 'bout for my birthday next year," he tried again.

"I can't promise," she said, turning back to her tortillas, "but we'll see."

Fausto walked back outside with a buttered tortilla. He knew his mother was right. His father was a warehouseman at Berven Rugs, where he made good money but not enough to buy everything his children wanted. Fausto decided to mow lawns to earn money, and was pushing the mower down the street before he realized it was winter and no one would hire him. He returned the mower and picked up a rake. He hopped onto his sister's bike (his had two flat tires) and rode north to the nicer section of Fresno in search of work. He went door-to-door, but after three hours he managed to get only one job, and not to rake leaves. He was asked to hurry down to the store to buy a loaf of bread, for which he received a grimy, dirt-caked quarter.

He also got an orange, which he ate sitting at the curb. While he was eating, a dog walked up and sniffed his leg. Fausto pushed him away and threw an orange peel skyward. The dog caught it and ate it in one gulp. The dog looked at Fausto and wagged his tail for more. Fausto tossed him a slice of orange, and the dog snapped it up and licked his lips.

"How come you like oranges, dog?"

The dog blinked a pair of sad eyes and whined.

"What's the matter? Cat got your tongue?" Fausto laughed at his joke and offered the dog another slice.

At that moment a dim light came on inside Fausto's head. He saw that it was sort of a fancy dog, a terrier or something, with dog tags and a shiny collar. And it looked well fed and healthy. In his neighborhood, the dogs were never licensed, and if they got sick they were placed near the water heater until they got well.

This dog looked like he belonged to rich people. Fausto cleaned his juice-sticky hands on his pants and got to his feet. The light in his head grew brighter. It just might work. He called the dog, patted its muscular back, and bent down to check the license.

"Great," he said. "There's an address."

The dog's name was Roger, which struck Fausto as weird because he'd never heard of a dog with a human name. Dogs should have names like Bomber, Freckles, Queenie, Killer, and Zero.

Fausto planned to take the dog home and collect a reward. He would say he had found Roger near the freeway. That would scare the daylights out of the owners, who would be so happy that they would probably give him a reward. He felt bad about lying, but the dog *was* loose. And it might even really be lost, because the address was six blocks away.

Fausto stashed the rake and his sister's bike behind a bush, and, tossing an orange peel every time Roger became distracted, walked the dog to his house. He hesitated on the porch until Roger began to scratch the door with a muddy paw. Fausto had come this far, so he figured he might as well go through with it. He knocked softly. When no one answered, he rang the doorbell. A man in a silky bathrobe and slippers opened the door and seemed confused by the sight of his dog and the boy.

"Sir," Fausto said, gripping Roger by the collar, "I found your dog by the freeway. His dog license says he lives here." Fausto looked down at the dog, then up to the man. "He does, doesn't he?"

The man stared at Fausto a long time before saying in a pleasant voice, "That's right." He pulled his robe tighter around him because of the cold and asked Fausto to come in. "So he was by the freeway?"

"Uh-huh."

"You bad, snoopy dog," said the man, wagging his finger. "You probably knocked over some trash cans, too, didn't you?"

Fausto didn't say anything. He looked around, amazed by this house with its shiny furniture and a television as large as the front window at home. Warm bread smells filled the air, and music full of soft tinkling floated in from another room.

"Helen," the man called to the kitchen, "we have a visitor." His wife came into the living room wiping her hands on a dish towel and smiling. "And who have we here?" she asked in one of the softest voices Fausto had ever heard.

"This young man said he found Roger near the freeway."

Fausto repeated his story to her while staring at a perpetual clock with a bell-shaped glass, the kind his aunt got when she celebrated her twenty-fifth anniversary. The lady frowned and said, wagging a finger at Roger, "Oh, you're a bad boy."

"It was very nice of you to bring Roger home," the man said. "Where do you live?"

"By that vacant lot on Olive," he said. "You know, by Brownie's Flower Place."

The wife looked at her husband, then Fausto. Her eyes twinkled triangles of light as she said, "Well, young man, you're probably hungry. How about a turnover?"

"What do I have to turn over?" Fausto asked, thinking she was talking about yard work or something like turning trays of dried raisins.

"No, no, dear, it's a pastry." She took him by the elbow and guided him to a kitchen that sparkled with copper pans and bright yellow wallpaper. She guided him to the kitchen table and gave him a tall glass of milk and something that looked like an *empanada*. Steamy waves of heat escaped when he tore it in two. He ate with both eyes on the man and woman who stood arm in arm smiling at him. They were strange, he thought. But nice.

"That was good," he said after he finished the turnover. "Did you make it, ma'am?"

"Yes, I did. Would you like another?"

"No, thank you. I have to go home now."

As Fausto walked to the door, the man opened his wallet and took out a bill. "This is for you," he said. "Roger is special to us, almost like a son."

Fausto looked at the bill and knew he was in trouble. Not with these nice folks or with his parents but with himself. How could he have been so deceitful? The dog wasn't lost. It was just having a fun Saturday walking around.

"I can't take that."

"You have to. You deserve it, believe me," the man said.

"No, I don't."

"Now don't be silly," said the lady. She took the bill from her husband and stuffed it into Fausto's shirt pocket. "You're a lovely child. Your parents are lucky to have you. Be good. And come see us again, please."

Fausto went out, and the lady closed the door. Fausto clutched the bill through his shirt pocket. He felt like ringing the doorbell and begging them to please take the money back, but he knew they would refuse. He hurried away, and at the end of the block, pulled the bill from his shirt pocket: it was a crisp twenty-dollar bill.

"Oh, man, I shouldn't have lied," he said under his breath as he started up the street like a zombie. He wanted to run to church for Saturday confession, but it was past four thirty, when confession stopped.

He returned to the bush where he had hidden the rake and his sister's bike and rode home slowly, not daring to touch the money in his pocket. At home, in the privacy of his room, he examined the twenty-dollar bill. He had never had so much money. It was probably enough to buy a secondhand guitar. But he felt bad, like the time he stole a dollar from the secret fold inside his older brother's wallet.

Fausto went outside and sat on the fence. "Yeah," he said. "I can probably get a guitar for twenty. Maybe at a yard sale—things are cheaper."

His mother called him to dinner.

The next day he dressed for church without anyone telling him. He was going to go to eight o'clock mass.

"I'm going to church, Mom," he said. His mother was in the kitchen cooking *papas* and *chorizo con huevos.* A pile of tortillas lay warm under a dishtowel.

"Oh, I'm so proud of you, son." She beamed, turning over the crackling *papas.*

His older brother, Lawrence, who was at the table reading the funnies, mimicked, "Oh, I'm so proud of you, my son," under his breath.

At Saint Theresa's he sat near the front. When Father Jerry began by saying that we are all sinners, Fausto thought he looked right at him. Could he know? Fausto fidgeted with guilt. No, he thought. I only did it yesterday.

Fausto knelt, prayed, and sang. But he couldn't forget the man and the lady, whose names he didn't even know, and the *empanada* they had given him. It had a strange name but tasted really good. He wondered how they got rich. And how that dome clock worked. He had asked his mother once how his aunt's clock worked. She said it just worked, the way the refrigerator works. It just did.

Fausto caught his mind wandering and tried to concentrate on his sins. He said a Hail Mary and sang, and when the wicker basket came his way, he stuck a hand reluctantly in his pocket and pulled out the twenty-dollar bill. He ironed it between his palms, and dropped it into the basket. The grownups stared. Here was a kid dropping twenty dollars in the basket while they gave just three or four dollars.

There would be a second collection for Saint Vincent de Paul, the lector announced. The wicker baskets again floated in the pews, and this time the adults around him, given a second chance to show their charity, dug deep into their wallets and purses and dropped in fives and tens. This time Fausto tossed in the grimy quarter.

Fausto felt better after church. He went home and played football in the front yard with his brother and some neighbor kids. He felt cleared of wrongdoing and was so happy that he played one of his best games of football ever. On one play, he tore his good pants, which he knew he shouldn't have been wearing. For a second, while he examined the hole, he wished he hadn't given the twenty dollars away.

Man, I coulda bought me some Levi's, he thought. He pictured his twenty dollars being spent to buy church candles. He pictured a priest buying an armful of flowers with *his* money.

Fausto had to forget about getting a guitar. He spent the next day playing soccer in his good pants, which were now his old pants. But that night during dinner, his mother said she remembered seeing an old bass *guitarron* the last time she cleaned out her father's garage.

"It's a little dusty," his mom said, serving his favorite enchiladas, "but I think it works. Grandpa says it works."

Fausto's ears perked up. That was the same kind the guy in Los Lobos played. Instead of asking for the guitar, he waited for his mother to offer it to him. And she did, while gathering the dishes from the table.

"No, Mom, I'll do it," he said, hugging her. "I'll do the dishes forever if you want."

It was the happiest day of his life. No, it was the second-happiest day of his life. The happiest was when his grandfather Lupe placed the *guitarron*, which was nearly as huge as a washtub, in his arms. Fausto ran a thumb down the strings, which vibrated in his throat and chest. It sounded beautiful, deep and eerie. A pumpkin smile widened on his face.

"OK, *hijo*, now you put your fingers like this," said his grandfather, smelling of tobacco and aftershave. He took Fausto's fingers and placed them on the strings. Fausto strummed a chord on the *guitarron*, and the bass resounded in their chests.

The *guitarron* was more complicated than Fausto imagined. But he was confident that after a few more lessons he could start a band that would someday play on *American Bandstand* for the dancing crowds.

The wind swept bitterly across the peak.

THE FIRE ON THE MOUNTAIN

Ethiopian folktale as told by
Harold Courlander and Wolf Leslau

People say that in the old days in the city of Addis Ababa there was a young man by the name of Arha. He had come as a boy from the country of Guragé, and in the city he became the servant of a rich merchant, Haptom Hasei.

Haptom Hasei was so rich that he owned everything that money could buy, and often he was very bored because he had tired of everything he knew, and there was nothing new for him to do.

One cold night, when the damp wind was blowing across the plateau, Haptom called to Arha to bring wood for the fire. When Arha was finished, Haptom began to talk.

"How much cold can a man stand?" he said, speaking at first to himself. "I wonder if it would be possible for a man to stand on the highest peak, Mount Sululta, where the coldest winds blow, through an entire night, without blankets or clothing, and yet not die?"

"I don't know," Arha said. "But wouldn't it be a foolish thing?"

"Perhaps, if he had nothing to gain by it, it would be a foolish thing to spend the night that way," Haptom said. "But I would be willing to bet that a man couldn't do it."

"I am sure a courageous man could stand naked on Mount Sululta throughout an entire night and not die of it," Arha said. "But as for me, it isn't my affair since I've nothing to bet."

"Well, I'll tell you what," Haptom said. "Since you are so sure it can be done, I'll make a bet with you anyway. If you can stand among the rocks on Mount Sululta for an entire night, without food or water or clothing or blankets or fire, and not die of it, then I will give you ten acres of good farmland for your own, with a house and cattle."

Arha could hardly believe what he had heard.

"Do you really mean this?" he asked.

"I am a man of my word," Haptom replied.

"Then tomorrow night I will do it," Arha said, "and afterward, for all the years to come, I shall till my own soil."

But he was very worried, because the wind swept bitterly across the peak. So in the morning Arha went to a wise old man from the Guragé tribe and told him of the bet he had made. The old man listened quietly and thoughtfully, and when Arha had finished he said:

"I will help you. Across the valley from Sululta is a high rock which can be seen in the daytime. Tomorrow night, as the sun goes down, I shall build a fire there, so that it can be seen from where you stand on the peak. All night long you must watch the light of my fire. Do not close your eyes or let the darkness creep upon you. As you watch my fire, think of its warmth, and think of me, your friend, sitting there tending it for you. If you do this, you will survive, no matter how bitter the night wind."

Arha thanked the old man warmly and went back to Haptom's house with a light heart. He told Haptom he was ready, and in the afternoon Haptom sent him, under the watchful eyes of other servants, to the top of Mount Sululta. There, as night fell, Arha removed his clothes and stood in the damp cold wind that swept across the plateau with the setting sun. Across the valley, several miles away, Arha saw the light of his friend's fire, which shone like a star in the blackness.

The wind turned colder and seemed to pass through his flesh and chill the marrow in his bones. The rock on which he stood felt like ice. Each hour the cold numbed him more, until he thought he would never be warm again, but he kept his eyes upon the twinkling light across the valley and remembered that his old friend sat there tending a

fire for him. Sometimes wisps of fog blotted out the light, and then he strained to see until the fog passed. He sneezed and coughed and shivered and began to feel ill. Yet all night through he stood there, and only when the dawn came did he put on his clothes and go down the mountain back to Addis Ababa.

Haptom was very surprised to see Arha, and he questioned his servants thoroughly.

"Did he stay all night without food or drink or blankets or clothing?"

"Yes," his servants said. "He did all of these things."

"Well, you are a strong fellow," Haptom said to Arha. "How did you manage to do it?"

"I simply watched the light of a fire on a distant hill," Arha said.

"What! You watched a fire? Then you lose the bet and you are still my servant and you own no land!"

"But this fire was not close enough to warm me, it was far across the valley!"

"I won't give you the land," Haptom said. "You didn't fulfill the conditions. It was only the fire that saved you."

Arha was very sad. He went again to his friend of the Guragé tribe and told him what had happened.

"Take the matter to the judge," the old man advised him.

Arha went to the judge and complained, and the judge sent for Haptom. When Haptom told his story, and the servants said once more that Arha had watched a distant fire across the valley, the judge said:

"No, you have lost, for Haptom Hasei's condition was that you must be without fire."

Once more Arha went to his old friend with the sad news that he was doomed to the life of a servant, as though he had not gone through the ordeal on the mountaintop.

"Don't give up hope," the old man said. "More wisdom grows wild in the hills than in any city judge."

He got up from where he sat and went to find a man named Hailu, in whose house he had been a servant when he was young.

He explained to the good man about the bet between Haptom and Arha, and asked if something couldn't be done.

"Don't worry about it," Hailu said after thinking for a while. "I will take care of it for you."

Some days later Hailu sent invitations to many people in the city to come to a feast at his house. Haptom was among them, and so was the judge who had ruled Arha had lost the bet.

When the day of the feast arrived, the guests came riding on mules with fine trappings, their servants strung out behind them on foot. Haptom came with

twenty servants, one of whom held a silk umbrella over his head to shade him from the sun, and four drummers played music that signified the great Haptom was here.

The guests sat on soft rugs laid out for them and talked. From the kitchen came the odors of wonderful things to eat: roast goat, roast corn and durra, pancakes called *injera*, and many tantalizing sauces. The smell of the food only accentuated the hunger of the guests. Time passed. The food should have been served, but they didn't see it, only smelled vapors that drifted from the kitchen. The evening came, and still no food was served. The guests began to whisper among themselves. It was very curious that the honorable Hailu had not had the food brought out. Still the smells came from the kitchen. At last one of the guests spoke out for all the others:

"Hailu, why do you do this to us? Why do you invite us to a feast and then serve us nothing?"

"Why, can't you smell the food?" Hailu asked with surprise.

"Indeed we can, but smelling is not eating, there is no nourishment in it!"

"And is there warmth in a fire so distant that it can hardly be seen?" Hailu asked. "If Arha was warmed by the fire he watched while standing on Mount Sululta, then you have been fed by the smells coming from my kitchen."

The people agreed with him; the judge now saw his mistake, and Haptom was shamed. He thanked Hailu for his advice, and announced that Arha was then and there the owner of the land, the house, and the cattle.

Then Hailu ordered the food brought in, and the feast began.

"This is too much," Gonta protested.

OOKA AND THE HONEST THIEF

Japanese folktale
as told by I. G. Edmonds

One day, Yahichi, owner of a rice store, came to Ooka's court, complaining that each night some of his rice disappeared.

"It is such a small amount that I hesitate to trouble your Honorable Honor," Yahichi said, touching the ground with his head to show proper respect for the great magistrate. "But I am reminded of the story of the mountain that was reduced to a plain because a single grain was stolen from it each day for centuries."

Ooka nodded gravely. "It is just as dishonest to steal one grain of rice as it is to steal a large sack," he remarked. "Did you take proper steps to guard your property?"

"Yes, my lord. I stationed a guard with the rice each night, but still it disappears. I cannot understand it," the rice merchant said, pulling his white beard nervously.

"What about your guard. Can he be trusted?" Ooka asked.

"Absolutely, Lord Ooka," Yahichi said. "The guard is Chogoro. He has served my family for seventy-five years."

"Yes, I know Chogoro," Ooka said. "He is a most conscientious man. He could not be the thief. But it is possible that he falls asleep at his post. After all, he is eighty years old."

"A man can be just as alert at eighty as at twenty," Yahichi replied quickly. "I am eighty-one myself, and I have never been so alert. Besides, I stood guard myself with Chogoro these last two nights. The rice vanished just the same."

"In that case I will watch with you tonight," Ooka said. "I should like to see this for myself."

As he had promised, Ooka made his way that evening to Yahichi's rice store. He was sure that both Yahichi and Chogoro had fallen asleep and had allowed the thief to enter each time the rice had been stolen, and it was not long before his suspicions were proved correct. Within an hour, both men were sleeping soundly. Ooka smiled. He was certain that when the men awoke neither would admit he had slept at all.

A little past midnight, Ooka heard a slight sound outside the building. He sprang to his feet and peered cautiously out the window. To his astonishment, Ooka found himself staring straight into the face of a man, standing in the shadows just outside the building. The judge recognized him as Gonta, a laborer who had been out of work for some time. The man was rooted to the spot by fear.

Ooka hesitated to arrest him. After all, he had not entered the rice store. Ooka would have no proof that he had come to steal. He could simply say that he had lost his way in the dark.

Though Ooka had recognized the thief, Gonta had not recognized the judge, for the darkness inside the building hid his face.

Ooka decided the best thing to do would be to pretend that he, too, was a thief. In this way he might trap Gonta into completing his crime. Speaking in a harsh tone to disguise his voice, he said, "You have obviously come here to steal rice just as I have."

Gonta was relieved to find himself face to face with another thief instead of a guard.

"As a favor from one thief to another," Ooka continued, "I will pass the rice out to you, so that you will not need to risk coming in yourself."

Gonta thanked him profusely for his courtesy, and Ooka picked up a large sack of rice and handed it out to him.

"This is too much," Gonta protested. "I want only a few handfuls."

Ooka was amazed. "But if you are going to steal, you may as well take a large amount. After all, if

Ooka catches you, you will be punished as much for stealing a single grain as you would for a whole sack."

"That would be dishonest!" Gonta replied indignantly. "I take just enough to feed my family for a single day, for each day I hope I will find work and not have to steal anymore. If I do find work, I intend to return all I have taken."

Then he took out the amount of rice he needed for his family's daily meal and handed the sack back to the astonished judge. Thanking Ooka once more for his courtesy, Gonta turned and disappeared into the darkness. Ooka did not try to stop him.

When the shopkeeper and his guard awoke, Ooka told them what had happened.

"But why did you let the thief go?" Yahichi asked indignantly.

"Gonta is certainly a thief," Ooka replied. "But I am convinced he is an honest one, for he refused to steal more than he needed."

"But, Lord Ooka, how can a man be a thief and honest at the same time?"

"I would never have believed it possible, but it is so," Ooka said. "It is the duty of a judge to punish wickedness and reward virtue. In this case, we find both qualities in the same man, so obviously it would be unfair to treat him as any ordinary thief."

"But, Lord Ooka—"

"I have made my decision. Tomorrow I will see that work is found for Gonta which is sufficient to feed his family and still leave enough to allow him to pay back the rice he stole. We will see if he keeps his promise. If he returns here and replaces the extra amount each night, it will prove my belief that he is an honest thief."

The plan was carried out according to Ooka's wishes. Gonta was given a job, without knowing that

Ooka was responsible. And, as the judge suspected, every night Gonta took the rice left over from his day's earnings and left it in the rice shop.

Ooka put all kinds of obstacles in his way to make it difficult for him to enter the shop, but this did not prevent Gonta from returning each night, although he became more and more afraid of being caught.

Yahichi admitted that the thief had been punished enough for his crime and told Ooka he did not wish to press charges. The great judge smiled and wrote out a small scroll which he ordered Yahichi to leave for Gonta to see when he came to pay for the last portion of rice.

When the honest thief slipped fearfully into the rice shop for the last time, he was shocked to find the scroll on which was written in Ooka's own handwriting, and bearing Ooka's signature, the following message:

You owe an extra ten percent for interest. Honesty is the best policy.

Theme Introduction

Perspective

In this section of the book, you will read stories about characters who see things in different ways, and characters who change how they look at things. Thinking about these stories, and about your own experiences, will give you new ideas about what it means to see things from a different perspective.

Important Questions to Think About

Before starting this section, think about your own experiences with perspective:

- Can you think of a time when your way of seeing things was different than someone else's? How did you feel about it? How did the other person feel?
- What helps you understand someone who has a different point of view?

Once you have thought about your own experiences with perspective, think about this **theme question** and write down your answers or share them aloud:

Why might someone try to see something from a different perspective?

After reading each story in this section, ask yourself the theme question again. You may have some new ideas you want to add.

There was an old woman who lived under a wave.

THE OLD WOMAN AND THE WAVE

Shelley Jackson

Once upon a time there was an old woman who lived under a wave. The wave never fell, but there was always the chance that it might, so every day the old woman went to the door of her cottage and looked out.

"Still there, wave?" she bellowed.

How could she know that the wave bent low when she yelled, just to hear her? The wave loved the old woman. But because the old woman had lived her whole life beneath it, she could see nothing good in the wave. She squinted for fear of a drop in the eye and hunched for fear of a drip down her collar. She never noticed the wave stretch its glassy body against the sun so the light was a blue-green shout in its stomach. She never saw the swallows wet their claws in the top of the wave and dare one another to fly under the tangled crest.

"How you can stand to live under that wave I'll never know," said the old man from down the road.

"Drip-drop," said the old woman. "I was born here and I'll die here."

In case the wave ever fell, the woman had built a little boat out of a washtub, a table leg, and an old apron. It had a cracked shovel for a rudder and an old broom for an oar. She kept it locked in a shed, and the key swung around her neck day and night.

All over her roof the old woman had fastened umbrellas of many colors and shapes and sizes. But no matter how hard she tried, she couldn't keep the wave from dripping and dropping, *fzzt* into the frying pan in the morning, *plunk* onto her pillow at night.

To make matters worse, old Bones, her dog, loved the wave. Sometimes she looked out of the cottage to see Bones, bubbles streaming from his muzzle, chasing fish in the belly of the wave. "Drip-drop," she said. "Shows how much sense you have."

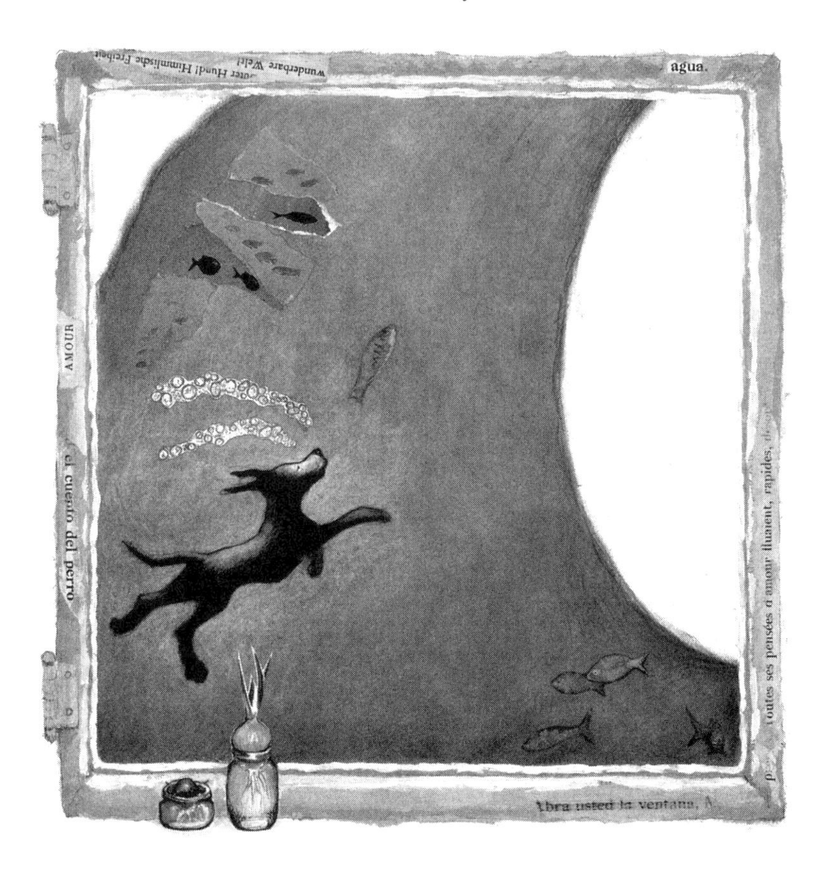

Often he slunk home wet from teeth to toenails. "Wicked Bones! Wicked wave!" she scolded.

A fish leaped from the wave and landed at her feet.

She picked it up and threw it back at the wave, which swallowed it. "Wasteful!" she roared. "Don't bother trying to soften me up!" And she slammed the door.

In the morning the light ran in liquid patterns across the walls of the old woman's cottage, and shadows of fish swam in at her window and across her blanket, waking her up. But the old woman just grumbled and turned her face to the wall. "I'll get up when I get up," she muttered. Yet a minute later her feet swung out of the covers and hunted for her slippers under the bed.

The old woman stepped out the door. "Still there, wave?" she yelled. The wave stood tall and shook itself, spattering her with drops. "Careless!" she said.

A fish leaped from the wave and landed wiggling in the grass at her feet. "Clumsy!" scolded the old woman, popping the fish in her apron to fry with butter and thyme for lunch.

She was picking pebbles out of the flower beds and tossing them back on the garden path when a wanderer rapped at the gate.

The stranger was young and strong and looking for work to do, so the old woman fed her on fish and sent her up to the roof to patch the umbrellas.

When she was done, the stranger sat on the chimney swinging her legs and looking up at the wave. She was whistling a strange little tune that made the old woman think of a bird flying in and out of a waterfall.

"Don't waste your time on that wave," the old woman called up sharply.

"That wave could take someone a long way, if someone wanted to go," said the wanderer, hopping off the chimney.

"You're welcome to it," said the old woman. "Take it with you when you go."

"I'd like to," said the wanderer wistfully as she climbed down the ladder. "But it's not the wave for me." She settled her hat and marched off down the gravel path.

The old woman rushed to the gate to look after her. "But where are you going?" she cried, for she had lived alone in the one house all her days.

"Away," said the wanderer, without looking back. "I just want to see . . ." She pointed down the road toward the blue and distant mountains, and, strangely, the old woman knew just what she meant. The old woman had never seen the mountains or the sea. She hobbled after her, but the stones hurt her bunions and the wanderer was already far ahead, and at last the old woman turned back.

"Drip-drop, at least I've got my Bones," she sighed, and cast her eye about. "Bones,"

she called. "Bones?" She whistled and clapped. "Bones!"

A smart smack of water landed on her forehead, firm as a kiss. "Why, you—" she said, and looked up, and then farther up, and farther still.

There was Bones, swimming high. He was up where the sun rode, up where the swallows fooled around in the spray.

"For shame!" she scolded the wave. But the wave stood like a statue as tall as the sky, Bones near the top of it. "Give me back my Bones," she roared to the wave, "or I'll tell the sun to dry you up, drip-drop!"

The old woman hurried to the shed with her little key and dragged out the boat. "I'll fetch that dog home," she muttered. She turned the boat over on her head and scurried to where the grass was always wet. There she set the boat against the side of the wave.

She rowed and heaved and strained up the wave till her shoulders ached and sweat ran off her arms.

At last, far ahead, she saw old Bones's ears against the sky.

"Bones!" she shouted. The dog swam back toward her, looking smug, but he let the old woman help him into the boat. "Where did you think you were off to?"

Bones wagged his wet tail.

The old woman wiped her face. She and the dog rested at the top of the wave, which murmured and sighed underneath them. The sun soothed her tired shoulders. Lights danced on the wave around her. The blue sky was close enough to touch, and the mountains just a splash and a plunge away.

She looked down at the house stuck all over with umbrellas. Suddenly the old woman laughed. "What a silly thing I am!" Bones wagged his tail again—*boom, boom, boom*—on the side of the washtub.

"Wave," the old woman said finally, pleased with herself. "I see, I see. But slowly, now!" The wave shimmered and a ripple went through it.

Then the wave lay down on the land.

Everything began to ripple and flow. The wave became a river, surging and plunging, swirling and curling, and flowing away, away, but never upsetting the boat in which Bones and the old woman rode.

Running after, the man from down the road cried, "But where are you going?"

"Away!" shouted the old woman. She didn't look back. She looked straight ahead at the mountains, and the waves that carried her toward them.

Papa and I rowed out on the Quabbin Reservoir.

LETTING SWIFT RIVER GO

Jane Yolen

AUTHOR'S NOTE

The Quabbin Reservoir is near my house,
one of the largest bodies of fresh water in
New England.
It is a lovely wilderness;
eagles soar overhead and deer mark out their paths.
But once it was a low-lying valley called Swift River,
surrounded by rugged hills.
There were towns in the valley filled with
hardworking folks
whose parents and grandparents had lived there all
their lives.
Then, between 1927 and 1946, all the houses

and churches and schools—the markers of
their lives—
were gone forever under the rising waters.

The drowning of the Swift River towns
to create the Quabbin was not a unique event.
The same story—only with different names—
has occurred all over the world
wherever nearby large cities have had
powerful thirsts.
Such reservoirs are trade-offs, which, like all trades,
are never easy, never perfectly fair.

When I was six years old
the world seemed a very safe place.
The wind whispered comfortably
through the long branches
of the willow by my bedroom window.
Mama let me walk to school all alone
along the winding blacktop,
past the Old Stone Mill,
past the Grange Hall,
past our church,
not even meeting up with
Georgie Warren or Nancy Vaughan
till the crossroads.

Georgie and I fished the Swift River
in the bright days of summer,
catching brown trout out of the pools
with a pin hook and a bit of thread.
We played mumblety-peg
in the graveyard
and picnicked on Grandpa Will's stone,
the black one that stayed warm all day
by soaking up the hot summer sun.

And many a summer night
I slept out under the backyard maples
with Nancy Vaughan.
We'd listen to the trains
starting and stopping along Rabbit Run,
their long whistles lowing into the dark,
startling the screech owl
off its perch on the great elm.
Lying there, looking up
at the lengthening shadows of trees,
we'd see the fireflies
winking on and off and on.

One night Nancy Vaughan
and her cousin Sara from the city
brought three mason jars to my house.
We caught fireflies in them,
holding our hands over the open tops.
Mama came out to watch.
She shook her head.
"You have to let them go, Sally Jane,"
she said to me.
So I did.

In the deep winter
Papa harvested ice
from Greenwich Lake,
and Mama kept the stove going
in the house all day and all night.
I slept under three eiderdowns
and Grandma's quilt.
Later, in March,
we put buckets up on all the maples,
dipping our fingers down into the sap
and tasting the thin sweetness.

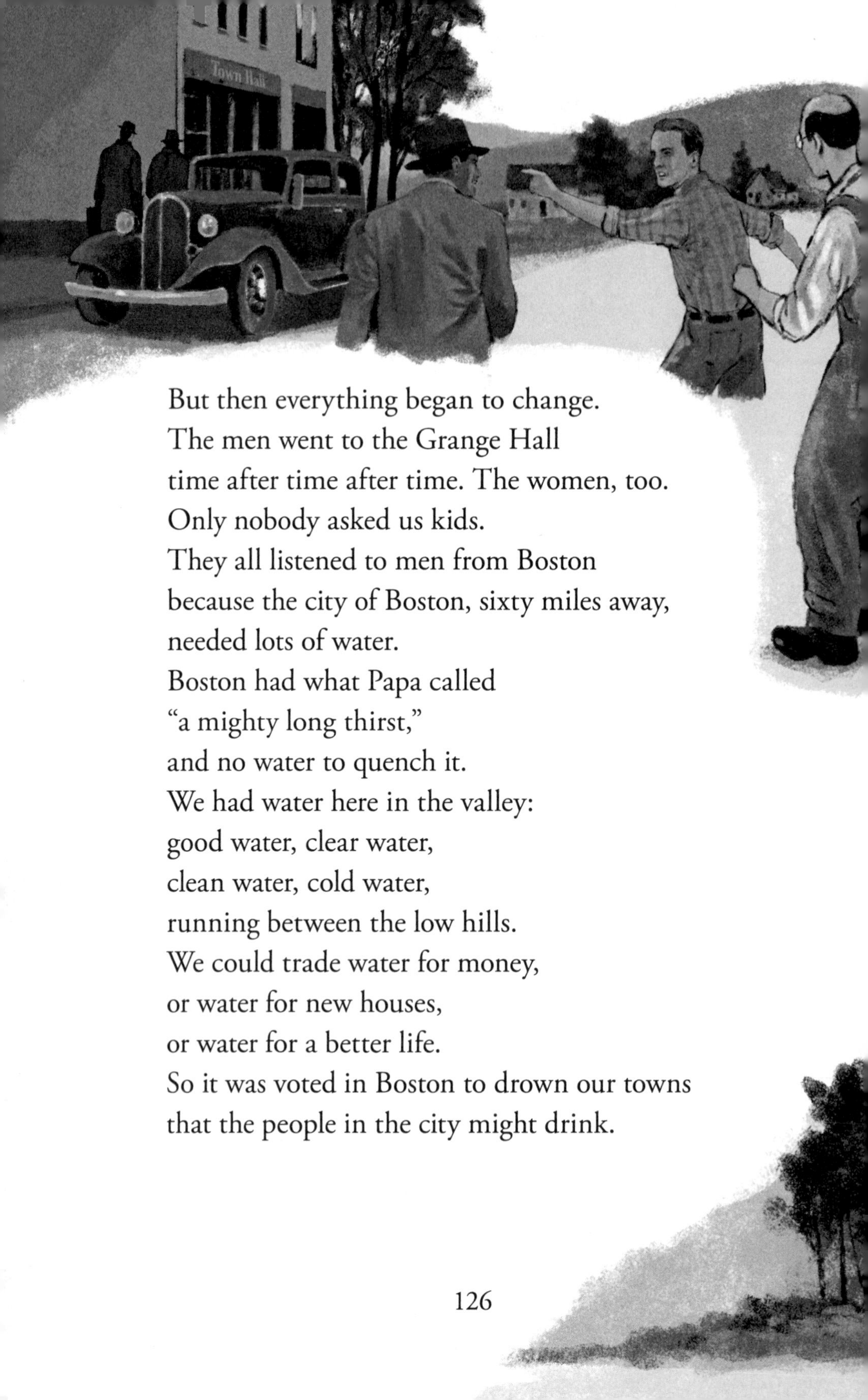

But then everything began to change.
The men went to the Grange Hall
time after time after time. The women, too.
Only nobody asked us kids.
They all listened to men from Boston
because the city of Boston, sixty miles away,
needed lots of water.
Boston had what Papa called
"a mighty long thirst,"
and no water to quench it.
We had water here in the valley:
good water, clear water,
clean water, cold water,
running between the low hills.
We could trade water for money,
or water for new houses,
or water for a better life.
So it was voted in Boston to drown our towns
that the people in the city might drink.

First we moved the graves:
Grandpa Will's black stone,
and the Doubledays and the Downings,
the Metcalfs and the Halls.
Papa read the headstones on the trucks
as he helped gather the small remains,
hauling them to the new cemetery
where everything would be fresh and green.
Sometimes all the men
found were buttons or teeth
or a few thin bones.
Papa said they left the Indians
where they lay.
No one wanted to bother with them,
but I thought it right
they remain in sacred ground.
The blackflies were fierce,
Papa said, fierce.
He had bites under his eyes,
swollen like tears.

Then the governor sent his “woodpeckers”
to clear the scrub and brush,
to cut down all the trees:
the maples and elms,
the willows and sycamores,
and the great spreading oaks.
They were stacked like drinking straws
along the roads,
then hauled away.

Our houses came next.
Some were bulldozed.
One great push and they went over
after one and two centuries
of standing strong
against wind and snow and rain.
Georgie and I watched them push down
the Old Stone Mill
till the windows of one wall
stared out like empty eyes
at the far-off hills.

Mr. Baxter's house went by truck
along the blacktop
to its new home in another town,
slow as any child going to school.
Nancy and I ran alongside for a ways,
but it had more breath than we did.
We stopped, panting,
and watched till it was out of sight.
Then Mama and Papa and I
moved away to New Salem,
one big hill over, and into a tiny house
where my room was warm all winter long.
Nancy and her folks went to the city
to be near her cousin Sara.
I never heard where Georgie went,
never even got to say goodbye.

Strangers came with their big machines,
building tunnels and caissons,
the Winsor Dam and the Goodnough Dike.
Papa brought me over to watch
most Friday afternoons.
"You've got to remember, Sally Jane," he said.
"Remember our town."
But it didn't *seem* like our town anymore.
There were no trees, no bushes,
no gardens, no fences,
no houses, no churches, no barns, no halls.
Just a long, gray wilderness,
just a hole between hills.

The water from the dammed rivers
moved in slowly and silently.
They rose like unfriendly neighbors
halfway up the sides of the hills,
covering Dana and Enfield,
Prescott and Greenwich,
all the little Swift River towns.
It took seven long years.

Much later, when I was grown,
Papa and I rowed out on the Quabbin Reservoir.
Behind us we left a bubble trail.
Through the late afternoon
and well into the evening
we sat in the little boat
and Papa pointed over the side.
"Look, Sally Jane," he said,
"that's where the road to Prescott ran,
there's the road to Beaver Brook,
that's the spot the church stood
where we had you baptized.
And the school.
And the Grange Hall.
And the Old Stone Mill.
We won't be seeing those again."
I looked.
I thought I could see the faint outlines,
but I could not read the past.
Little perch now owned those streets,
and bass swam over the country roads.
A rainbow trout leaped after a fly,
and the water rings rippled through
my father's careful mapping.

When it got dark
the stars came out,
reflecting in the water,
winking on and off and on like fireflies.
I leaned over the side of the boat
and caught the starry water
in my cupped hands.
For a moment I remembered
the wind through the willow,
the trains whistling on Rabbit Run,
the crossroads where I had met
Georgie Warren and Nancy Vaughan.
Gone, all gone, under the waters.

Then I heard my mother's voice
coming to me over the drowned years.
"You have to let them go, Sally Jane."
I looked down into the darkening deep,
smiled,
and did.

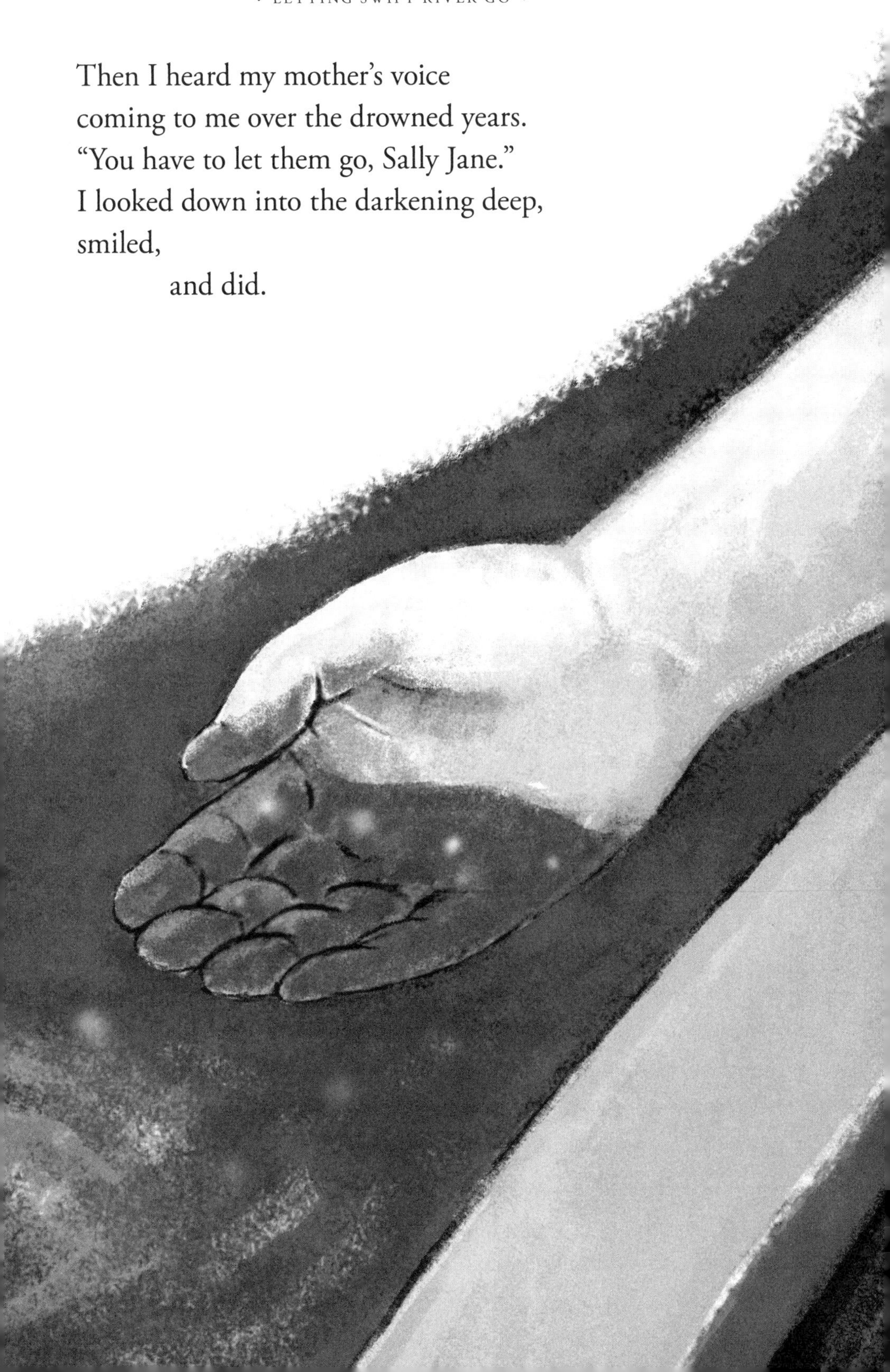

Her name was Myra White.

The Apple and the Envelope

Herbert Montgomery

PART 1

Her name was Myra White, and she came to our school right after Christmas last year. She was sort of different looking. I mean if somebody asked you what Myra looked like, you wouldn't know what to say. Except maybe that she had black hair. And she always wore a green sweater.

The girls in our class are awful fussy about the clothes people wear. Especially Joyce. She's got a secret club, and the girls who belong to it have to dress in a certain way. And they have a way of insulting people that they think is so smart. The minute I saw Myra walk into our room I knew Joyce wouldn't like her.

Our teacher, Mrs. Peters, gave Myra the desk way back in the corner. Every day Myra just sat there, and I can't remember her ever saying anything worth remembering.

One day on our way to school my friend Joey and I were fooling around with his little brother's old Creepy Crawler. Joey had it tied to a string, and he was swinging it around. He kept yelling, "Raaawwg!" at me every time he bounced the crawler in my face. It made me kind of mad so I had to think of a way to make him quit.

The crawler looked sort of like an octopus and sort of like a spider. Girls don't much like spiders. That gave me a great idea. "Let's put the crawler in Myra's desk," I said.

"What for?" Joey asked.

"To scare her into talking," I said. "I bet she would jump right out of her seat."

"Or maybe scream," Joey said, and I could tell he was getting to like the idea.

Joey untied the string and flipped the crawler to me. "You can do it," he said.

"You do it," I said, flipping it back.

"What's the matter? You scared?"

"I'm not scared," I said, catching the crawler as Joey threw it to me. He stuck his hands in his pockets. I knew if I threw the crawler back to him again he'd just leave it on the sidewalk. "Okay," I said, "I'll do it."

We had to wait until noon when everybody was gone for lunch. Joey and I sneaked back to the room and then put the crawler in Myra's desk. We could hardly wait for everybody to come back to the room. And we could hardly wait for Myra to take a book out of her desk. Man! She sure would scream or something, then.

When we were all in class after the noon bell, I kept looking over to see what was going to happen. Then I got tired of waiting and started to do some reading.

I forgot all about the crawler until I heard Mrs. Peters walking away from her desk. She walked back to where Myra sat. Myra had her head down on her desk. I couldn't hear what Mrs. Peters whispered to her. Whatever it was, Myra just got up and walked out. Mrs. Peters hurried after her and the last thing she said was, "I don't want to hear one word from this classroom!"

It was quiet for a little while. Then it just seemed like everybody started talking at once. We all got louder and louder. I took a chance on getting back the crawler. I was lucky enough to make it back to my seat before Mrs. Peters came into the room again. She really gave it to us.

On our way home that night, I gave the crawler to Joey and he said, "Myra must be some kind of nut. I know she looked in her desk. And she didn't say a word."

"Maybe she wasn't feeling good," I said. "Do you think she went to see the nurse?"

"I don't know," Joey said.

After that I forgot about Myra until the next morning when we were back inside the school playground. Mostly we were just fooling around. Myra was standing by herself over beside the building. She was still wearing her old green sweater. It seemed like she wore that sweater just about every day.

And then I got my idea. I told it to Joey and he thought it was a good idea, too. So then we went around and told everybody else in our class.

When the bell rang, we all waited for Myra to go in. We wanted to be sure she had time to get to her desk. Then we followed her. Instead of going right to our own places, we all walked way to the back of the room so we could go past Myra. One by one, we said good morning in a super-sweet way.

"**GOOD MORNING, MYRA**," I said and I pressed my lips tight to hold back a laugh.

"Good morning, MYRA," Joey whispered. He nodded his head as though he was speaking to a queen.

The girls behind us sounded like singers getting in tune.

"Good morning, Myra."

"*Good morning, Myra.*"

"**Good morning, Myra.**"

"GOOD MORNING, MYRA."

It went on and on. I guess Mrs. Peters was too surprised to do anything but sit behind her desk with her mouth open. Myra looked pretty surprised, too. None of us had ever talked so politely to her before. There were a few snickers as the last kids in the line took their places, but Mrs. Peters stopped all sound with just one look. I sat quietly looking into a book so I didn't have to watch any more.

Later, at recess, we were all outside choosing sides for a game. Nobody wanted Myra. Patty and Leo were choosing. When there was just Myra left, Patty and Leo began to argue about who had to take Myra. While they both were still arguing, Myra walked back into the school. We played without her.

That was kind of the way things went all the time last year. Whenever we lined up to get a drink at the fountain, Myra was always last. When we had to choose sides, she was always last. She was last in gym. At noon she sat someplace by herself and ate her lunch from a paper bag.

For our Valentine's Day party we had it all fixed so that nobody would give Myra a valentine. Joyce and all her friends kept giggling about it, so Mrs. Peters put them in charge of making the valentine box. She had them work on a table near her desk. They used about a ton of paper to cover a cardboard box with red and white hearts. Every once in a while you could hear Joyce giggling. You can tell her voice almost a mile away. Then Mrs. Peters would look slowly around the room at everybody until it was quiet again.

All the time I kept thinking about our plan. But whenever I sneaked a look at Myra, it didn't seem so funny. She always sat with her head bent over a book, and her hands beside her face in a way that made her look real sad. I knew Mrs. Peters wouldn't like what we were going to do.

So after supper the night before Valentine's Day, I went down to the drugstore to look for a card to give to Myra. I waited around until nobody I knew was in the store. Then I bought one of those fifty-cent valentines with the satin on the front and everything. It sure smelled like a valentine for a girl.

When I got home, I had to hide the card. Mom would start to ask a lot of questions if she saw me with a valentine like that.

For a long time that night I sat in my bedroom thinking about Myra. We hadn't ever had anyone quite like her in our class before. It seemed that no matter what we did, she didn't do anything back. I kept thinking and looking at the valentine and trying to decide if I should really give it to her. If anybody in the class found out, they'd be down on me for sure.

It bothered me to see that valentine just lie there on the table. I couldn't take it back. I couldn't send it to anybody else. So right then I made up my mind to really do it. I printed Myra's name right on the envelope. I tried to do it in a way so nobody could tell it was from me. Then I was stuck. I thought and thought about what to write on the inside. I sure didn't want to put my name there.

At last I decided to write:

From a friend

The next day, after the party, Joey was real mad. "Somebody spoiled all the fun," he said.

"Yeah," I said. "Someone sure did."

It was about a month after that when Myra moved away. Mrs. Peters told us that Myra's father was a construction worker. He had to move to a new place where there was more work in the winter, and he took the whole family along.

It was kind of spooky around school after Myra left. It was all because of the apple. I had seen Myra come in early and give it to Mrs. Peters that last day she came to school. The next morning the apple was on the corner of Mrs. Peters' desk. It was one of those extra-big delicious apples. Almost as big as a softball. There was an envelope beside the apple. I felt kind of hot all over and worried when I saw what it said on the envelope:

For about a week the apple stood there all shiny. Just like you could taste the juice in your mouth. Then it began drying out. The shine was gone. The apple got drier and smaller and drier and smaller.

Mrs. Peters kept that apple and card on her desk for a long time. Joey and I talked about the apple just about every day. Joey always said, "She sure did get even with us. I wish I knew who gave her that valentine."

"Yeah. So do I," was all I could ever say. But I still keep wondering what the kids are like wherever Myra is now. And I sure would like to know what was inside that envelope.

PART 2

My mother and I were in the bedroom unpacking boxes. When I looked out the window and saw kids playing, I felt the way I always feel when I have to

start going to another strange school. “Can’t I just stay home?” I asked, wishing my mother would say that I never had to go to school again.

“Myra, you have to go to school,” my mother said. She kept on taking things out of boxes and putting them away. “And why would you want to stay home all day when you can be with children your own age?”

“Nobody likes me,” I said.

“Oh, Myra! That’s not true! Lots of people like you.”

“No they don’t!”

My mother stopped hanging clothes in the closet and sat on the edge of the bed beside me. “I like you,” she said, “and Daddy likes you—” Before she could finish, I said, “That’s different.”

"How is it different?"

"Relatives *have* to like you."

Mother put her arms around me and I sort of leaned against her, biting my lips hard so I wouldn't cry. I was sure she couldn't understand what it felt like to change schools so often. I'd gone to so many schools in so many different towns that I couldn't even remember them all. "I don't ever want to get to know anybody," I said. "Even if I made friends, we'd just move away, and I'd never see them again."

"I know how you must feel," my mother said softly. "But if we didn't move, your father would be out of work. And I thought you liked your last school. I can remember that nice valentine you got."

"No one even signed it!" I said angrily. "It was just a big joke!"

"Nobody makes jokes like that."

"Yes they do, Mother. They do; they *do*! They make jokes like that about me!"

Mother went on talking to me, but I wasn't even listening. All I could think about was last year. Last year and Lincoln School, where I started right after Christmas.

When I first walked into the room, Mrs. Peters smiled at me. I thought then that it might be different this time, but it wasn't. She gave me a desk in a back corner of the room. I bet if they had a desk in the hall, they would have put me there. Just on the outside of everything.

Right away trouble started. I hadn't studied half the things everybody else seemed to know. And when Mrs. Peters asked me questions, I didn't know the answers.

It was always like that.

After lunch one day a girl named Joyce came up to talk to me. At first I thought she wanted to be my friend. Instead she talked about somebody she called Anna-Marie. "Don't you think that Anna-Marie is dumb?" she asked.

I didn't know what to say, but I wanted Joyce to like me. So I nodded my head even though I didn't know Anna-Marie.

"She never knows the answer to anything," Joyce said. Real snotty-like. "And her hair looks like rats live in it. She always wears the same ugly sweater, too." Joyce looked up and down the hallway before whispering in my ear, "*Nobody* in the whole school likes her."

Having Joyce come up and talk to me made me feel a little happy. But that only lasted until recess when I heard her talking to some other girls in the hall. I heard Joyce giggle as she said, "Can you imagine! Myra didn't even know I was talking to her about herself!" They all giggled like it was really funny.

After that, I hated to wear my green sweater. It was the nicest sweater I had. My dad had given it to me for my birthday and until then I'd been very proud of it. No matter what Joyce said, I wasn't going to stop wearing that sweater.

Things went on like that all the time I was at Lincoln. Joyce and her friends had a club. They only let people in that they liked. Well, I sure wasn't in the club.

One other time when we were all back in the room after lunch, I opened my desk to take out a book. I didn't look inside. As I reached in, I felt this awful thing with legs all over it. I just about screamed, but I didn't dare. I swallowed hard and peeked into the desk. Somebody had put this dumb creepy thing on top of my books. I knew then that everybody was going to be mean to me and I put my head down on my desk. I felt sick.

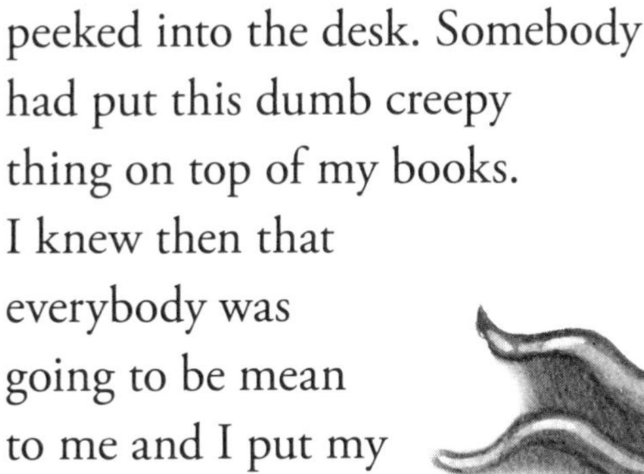

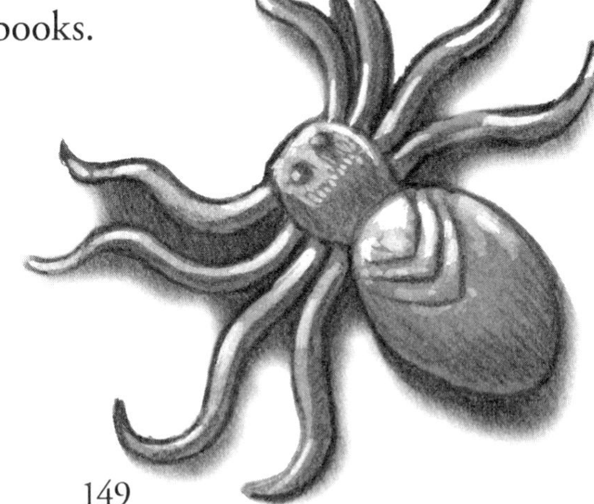

Mrs. Peters came over to my desk and talked in such a kind way that I knew I was going to cry. I couldn't stand to have the class see me, so when I felt my eyes get wet I got up and ran out of the room. I almost fell on the steps as I raced away from the school.

I took the shortest way home, through the park. When I came to a tree, I hid behind it. I leaned my forehead against the rough bark and pounded it with my fists. "I hate you, hate you!" I yelled at the tree. And for a long time I stayed in the park.

Later, at home, I told my mother I had a stomachache. She made me go to bed.

Things like this were always happening to me. After a while I couldn't seem to read a book or do any of the work I was supposed to do. It wasn't long before Mrs. Peters stopped calling on me in class.

Recess was the time I hated most. I can hit a ball better than most boys. But the boys never want you to play ball when you're as good as they are. So we play all those other dumb games. It's worse in a boy-girl game where you have to choose sides. Everybody stands around and two leaders choose. They always pick the best first. It's not so bad when they pick the first few people, because you're still standing in a big bunch. But when it gets close to the end, you can tell the people nobody wants on their side. I used to imagine that if I ever got to be the leader I would pick the poorest player first. I wouldn't care if my side lost. I'd make the good players know what it was like to not always be first. But that's only a dream, and dreams don't come true just by wishing.

I think Valentine's Day is the worst day of the year. It's icky. I always try to think of some excuse to stay home that day so I don't have to watch everybody opening valentines. When I was going to the Lincoln School, my mother bought me a whole box of valentines. I put them all in the envelopes, but I only wrote a name on one to give Mrs. Peters. I had that one on top of the pile so that Mother wouldn't know the rest weren't for anybody. Then on my way to school I dumped all but the one on top in somebody else's garbage can out behind the building where we lived.

When it was time for the party, I sat in my place like a stone, dreading the time the heart-covered box was opened. Of course everybody got just gobs of silly valentines and I sat there with only one. I knew it was from Mrs. Peters. She would give one to everybody. And I knew her writing.

Joyce passed out the valentines. When she put a second one on my desk, I could hardly believe my eyes. She looked as though she couldn't believe it either, so I knew for sure it wasn't from her or anybody in her club. I opened the valentine from Mrs. Peters and slipped the other one in my notebook.

That afternoon I rushed home. I was pounding all over, trying to imagine who the valentine could be from. When I got home, I hurried to my bedroom and closed the door. I opened my notebook slowly, thinking I might have imagined the other valentine. But it was still there!

I opened it carefully. It was the prettiest valentine I'd ever seen anybody give to anybody in school. I felt warm all over. On the inside the card said:

From a friend

I felt like I was going to choke. It looked like a boy's printing, but I couldn't be sure. I didn't really care. Someone liked me! I felt soft all over. I wanted to sing. I wanted to cry. I guess the only time I ever felt like that before was when my dad gave me my green sweater. Everything seemed beautiful.

School was lots better after that. Sometimes I smiled at kids when I walked down the hall. I couldn't ever be sure that the person I smiled at might not be my friend. But no one ever acted like a friend. And then about a month after Valentine's Day, we had to move again.

I guess Lincoln was the first school that I didn't really want to leave. It seemed that if I could stay through the year, things might be better in the fall. But we had to go.

I worried about leaving without letting my secret friend know how happy I was. So one night I wrote a letter. It was pretty silly I guess. But there were lots of things I wanted to say and I wrote them all down. Then, on my way to school, I stopped in the small

store where lots of the kids who go to Lincoln stop to buy candy and gum. I bought a big apple, the nicest one there was. The delicious kind I like so much. I got to school early, and gave the apple and letter to Mrs. Peters. She asked me lots of questions and told me how nice she thought I was. That was hard to believe.

It was sure nice to leave school at noon that day and not have to eat my lunch alone.

So that was the end of going to Lincoln School. And now we've moved and I've got to start all over again.

"Myra." It was my mother calling gently. "You've been daydreaming."

I sat up beside her and looked at the boxes of stuff that still had to be unpacked. "I was just thinking about my old school," I said.

"Things will be different in this one," my mother said. I didn't want to argue with her, but how could she know?

"Maybe," I said, reaching down to unfold the flaps of another box. Maybe things will be different in this school, but I doubt it.

As I walked to the closet to hang up my green sweater, I looked out the window at the kids playing on the sidewalk. They looked like the kids at Lincoln. I hope my friend didn't laugh when he read my letter.

A Guide to Question Types

Below are different types of questions you might ask while reading. Notice that it isn't always important (or even possible) to answer all questions right away. The questions below are about "Tuesday of the Other June" (pp. 15–33).

Factual questions are about the story and have one correct answer that you can find by looking back at the story.	How do the two Junes know each other? (Answer: The two girls meet at the community center swimming pool.) Why doesn't June's mother know about the Other June? (Answer: June's mother doesn't know because June never tells her.)
Vocabulary questions are about words or phrases in the story. They can be answered with the glossary (pp. 161–179), a dictionary, or *context clues*—parts of the story near the word that give hints about its meaning.	Is a "bureau" the same as a dresser? What does "good riddance" mean? (Practice finding context clues on page 24 to figure out the meaning of this phrase.)
Background questions are often about a story's location, time period, or culture. You can answer them with information from a source like the Internet or an encyclopedia.	What things can you do at a community center? How do you get to be an apartment caretaker?

Speculative questions ask about events or details that are not covered in the story. You must guess at or invent your answers.

Where did June's father go?

Will the Other June ever try to bully June again?

Evaluative questions ask for your personal opinion about something in the story, like whether a character does the right thing. These questions have more than one good answer. Support for these answers comes from your beliefs and experiences as well as the story.

Should someone in the swimming class have told the teacher that the Other June was bullying June?

Is June's mother right that if you smile at the world, "the world'll surely smile back"?

Interpretive questions ask about the deep meaning of the story and are the focus of a Shared Inquiry discussion. They have more than one good answer. Support for these answers comes only from evidence in the story.

Why is June finally able to say "no more" to the Other June?

Why does the Other June start picking on June?

Shared Inquiry Beyond the Classroom

The skills you have practiced in Junior Great Books will help you in school, but they will also help you in other parts of your life. Through your practice with Shared Inquiry you've learned to:

Ask questions. To learn almost anything, you need to ask questions. If you want to know how to program a computer, play chess, or bake a cake, questions can help you understand what to do and why. The first step to understanding is expressing what you don't understand, and asking questions to find out more helps you learn something *really* well.

Think deeply and search for meaning. By discussing stories, you've learned that you can understand more by going deeper. Lots of things in life are like this, such as movies, art, and the natural world. Spending time looking closely at things and wondering about them helps you understand more about the world around you.

Back up your ideas with evidence. Being able to develop your ideas and support them with evidence are important skills. When you write an essay, give a speech, or even ask for more allowance, you need to be able to say clearly what your idea is and why you think it's reasonable.

Listen and respond to others' ideas. Even if your first idea about a story is a good one, listening to other people's ideas can help you better understand what you think. You may find new ways to support your idea, or you may change your mind. This will help you with many things in life, like deciding what sports team to join or who to vote for in an election.

Respect other people's points of view. In Junior Great Books, you've seen that two people can read the same story and have different ideas about it without one person having to be wrong. You have also learned to agree and disagree with others politely. These skills will help you get along with others in all parts of your life.

Glossary

In this glossary, you'll find definitions for words that you may not know but are in the stories you've read. You'll find the meaning of each word as it is used in the story. The word may have other meanings as well, which you can find in a dictionary if you're interested. If you don't find a word here that you are wondering about, go to your dictionary for help.

abrupt: Sudden. *When my dad pulled the plug on the stereo, the music came to an **abrupt** end.*

accentuated: To **accentuate** something is to call special attention to it. *The baby deer's long eyelashes **accentuated** its big eyes.*

adjust, adjustment: To **adjust** to something is to become more and more used to it. *It might take you a few weeks to **adjust** to a new school or a new baby in the family.* An **adjustment** is a change you make to get used to something. *You would make an **adjustment** to a different way of life if you moved from the country to the city.*

affair: If something is your **affair**, it's your business. *What I write in my diary is my **affair**—nobody else is allowed to read it.*

Bach: Johann Sebastian Bach, a famous German composer of classical music from the 1700s.

bellowed: To **bellow** means to shout something in a deep, loud voice. *The coach **bellowed** instructions to the players from the sidelines.* To **bellow** also means to make a deep, loud noise. *When he stubbed his toe he **bellowed** in pain.*

besieged: To **besiege** a city is to surround it with enemy forces so that no one can get out or in. *The king and his men planned a way to escape the **besieged** castle.*

bunions: Large and painful bumps that grow on the big toes.

bureau: A chest of drawers or a dresser.

caissons: Waterproof structures built so that construction work can be done under water.

charges: A **charge** is an official statement saying that someone has done something illegal or wrong. When you **press charges**, you officially blame a person for committing a crime. *My neighbor wants to **press charges** against the man who broke her window and take him to court.*

charity: Money or help given freely to those who need it. *He showed his **charity** by working at the local food pantry.*

***chorizo con huevos*:** Spanish for "sausage with eggs."

clustered: Things that **cluster** are gathered close together or stand near each other. *The town's tallest buildings **clustered** around the main square.*

conditions: A **condition** is something that must happen before another thing can happen. *My father says we can watch a movie on two **conditions**: that we do our homework first and that we don't stay up too late.*

confession: In church, **confession** is the time when people tell their sins to the priest.

***conjunto* music:** A kind of music popular in Texas and Mexico, featuring an accordion and a kind of guitar called a *bajo sexto. Conjunto* is Spanish for "together."

conscientious: If you are **conscientious**, you know right from wrong, and you do what you think is right. *A **conscientious** student would not cheat on a test.* Being **conscientious** also means taking the time to do things carefully and completely. *I was **conscientious** and double-checked my homework for spelling mistakes.*

courtesy: Politeness and thoughtfulness; showing good manners. *You show **courtesy** when you write thank-you notes for your birthday presents.*

crest: The **crest** of a mountain, hill, or wave is the very top of it. *When the climbers reached the **crest** of the hill, they looked down at the fields below.*

croon: A soft song or a hum. *A **croon** and some gentle rocking might put a baby to sleep.*

daze: If you are in a **daze**, you are stunned and confused by something. *She was **dazed** after hearing the shocking news of the accident.*

deceitful: Someone who lies to or tricks others is **deceitful**. *If you tried to blame your brother for something you did, you would be **deceitful**.*

devoted: To be **devoted** is to give something or someone all your time and attention. *My friend is **devoted** to chess and spends all of her recess time practicing.*

dismissed: To be **dismissed** is to be told to go away, or to be allowed to go. *We always have to wait to be **dismissed** from the table when we are done eating dinner.*

distracted: If you are **distracted**, you are not focused on what you are doing because something else has your attention. *It's easy to get **distracted** from your homework if the television is on at the same time.*

distribution: Handing things out or dividing things among a group. *The teacher put a student in charge of the* ***distribution*** *of tests to everyone in the class.*

doomed: When you are **doomed**, you are certain to have terrible or unfortunate things happen to you. *People living close to where the fire started were* ***doomed*** *to lose their houses. A very nasty person might be* ***doomed*** *to live the rest of his life without any friends.*

dreading: To **dread** something means to wait for it with great fear or unhappiness. *She sat in the dentist's chair,* ***dreading*** *the moment he might find a cavity.*

droning: To **drone** is to speak in a flat and boring voice. ***Droning*** *on and on, the speaker almost put the class to sleep.*

durra: The African name for a type of grain grown in many warm parts of the world.

eerie: Strange or spooky. *There were* ***eerie*** *noises coming from inside the haunted house at the fair.*

eiderdowns: Quilts stuffed with the feathers of an *eider* duck (a large sea duck).

***empanada*:** A Spanish or Latin American pastry with a meat or vegetable filling.

exchanges: An **exchange** is a trade of one thing for another. *The new neighbor and I have had a few* ***exchanges*** *of smiles, but no conversation yet.*

fidgeted: To **fidget** is to move around in an uneasy or nervous way. *The girl **fidgeted** in her seat until her father told her to keep still.*

flannel: A type of soft cloth made from wool and other material.

flings: To **fling** something is to throw it hard. *When she **flings** the frisbee toward the lake, her dog goes running after it.*

frisky: Full of energy and playfulness. *Whenever my dad puts on salsa music, my sister and I get **frisky** and start to dance.*

fulfill: To **fulfill** means to meet a duty or a required task. *You won't get a part in the play if you can't **fulfill** the requirement to rehearse every day.* **Fulfill** also means to carry out or finish something. *If you do get a part in the play, you'll **fulfill** your dream to act onstage.*

funnies: Another name for the comics in a newspaper.

fusillade: A fast string of explosions from a gun or cannon.

fussy: A **fussy** person may be hard to please, and pays a lot of attention to the details of things that may not matter very much. *My **fussy** little brother always has to drink out of his blue cup or he starts crying. My aunt is **fussy** about how we set the table—we have to put the silverware in exactly the right place.*

good riddance: Saying "**good riddance**" means you are glad that something you don't like is going away or out of your sight. *You might say "**good riddance**" if you found out your loud, rude neighbors were moving.*

gravely: When you do something **gravely**, you do it in a very serious way. *The man listened **gravely** to the news of the car accident.*

grimy: Dirty.

***guitarron*:** A kind of large bass guitar.

hauling, hauled: To **haul** something means to pull or drag it with force. *The men were **hauling** the heavy tree branches away by tying ropes to them and pulling them behind a truck.*

headstones: A piece of stone that marks where someone is buried. ***Headstones** often have the person's name, date of birth, and date of death written on them.*

heaved: To **heave** is to lift or push something that is hard to move. *We watched the construction crew as they **heaved** a huge load of bricks onto the sidewalk.*

***hijo*:** Spanish for "son."

hobbled, hobbles: To **hobble** a horse is to tie its legs together with ropes or straps to keep it from getting loose. These ropes or straps are called **hobbles**. *We **hobbled** the horses because we don't have a stable for them.* To **hobble** also means to limp or walk stiffly, usually from pain. *The girl with the broken leg **hobbled** to school on her crutches each day.*

honorable: Showing a sense of what is right and proper. *You would be **honorable** if you told the truth even if you knew it might get you into trouble.* The word **honorable** is also sometimes used before an important person's name to show respect.

huffing: Someone is **huffing** if they are breathing or blowing very hard. *She was **huffing** by the time she walked all the way up the hill.*

indignantly: If you say or do something **indignantly**, you are upset and angry because you feel that you have not been treated fairly. *She stomped off to her room **indignantly** when her parents punished her for something she didn't do.*

interest: An extra amount of money that must be paid when someone borrows money. *If the bank lends her money to buy a house, she will need to pay the bank back all the money plus some **interest**.*

intuition: You use your **intuition** when you figure something out mostly by using your feelings. *The hunter's **intuition** told him that there was a deer nearby.*

ivory: A hard, smooth, white material that forms the tusks of elephants. ***Ivory*** *is sometimes used to make expensive objects such as jewelry and small statues.*

lector: Someone who reads aloud during a church service.

littered: A place or surface that is **littered** is covered with things, often trash, in an untidy way. *Her room was* ***littered*** *with dirty clothes and candy wrappers.*

lodge: A type of Native American house. *One type of* ***lodge*** *is a* wigwam, *which is often shaped like a dome and made with bark or animal skins.*

loo-loos: Loud, high-pitched sounds made by Plains Indian women to celebrate something good happening.

magistrate: A judge.

mahogany: A reddish-brown wood that comes from tropical trees.

marrow: The soft material that fills the inside of bones.

merchant: A person who buys and sells things for a living. *There is a jewelry* ***merchant*** *at the mall who sells pretty necklaces.* A **merchant** can also be the owner or manager of a store. *All the* ***merchants*** *in town decorate their shop windows during the holidays.*

mimicked: To copy someone or something, usually in order to make fun of them. *My sister **mimicked** my brother's voice to make me laugh.*

mission: A **mission** is a very important goal or job, usually one that takes a long time to finish. *He made it his **mission** to get his favorite musician's autograph by the end of the year.*

mortars: Guns that fire bombs high into the air.

mounted: To **mount** an animal is to climb on its back. *The man **mounted** his horse and rode away quickly.*

mumblety-peg: An old-fashioned game in which players throw a sharp stick or knife to try to make it stick into the ground.

murmur: A **murmur** is a soft, low, hard-to-hear sound made by a person or group of people. *The **murmur** of voices from the party in the basement barely reached the living room.*

muzzle: The long front part of some animals' faces (like horses or dogs), including the nose and mouth. *The puppy stuck its **muzzle** into the bowl and sniffed at the food inside.*

nourishment: The food and other things you need to live and grow in a healthy way. *Junk food is fun to eat, but it will give you very little **nourishment**.*

obstacles: An **obstacle** is something that gets in your way or stops you from doing something easily. *The biggest **obstacle** to getting his homework done was that he had forgotten his book at school.*

obvious: Something **obvious** is clear or easy to understand. *From the way that he shouted it was **obvious** that he was upset.*

ordeal: An **ordeal** is a difficult or painful experience or test. *If you broke your arm falling out of a tree and had to get a cast, you might describe the experience as an **ordeal**.*

pallet: A small, hard bed that often has a straw-filled mattress.

***papas*:** Spanish for "potatoes."

perch: A **perch** is the place where a bird sits, like the branch of a tree or the top of a building. *The pigeons fell asleep on their **perch** in the oak tree.* A **perch** is also a kind of fish that lives in lakes and rivers.

perpetual clock: A type of clock that keeps perfect time and winds itself using changes in temperature and weather.

pews: Benches that people sit on in church.

pierced: When something sharp or pointed **pierces** something else, it goes into or through it. *The sharp knife **pierced** the tough meat with no trouble.* A sound that **pierces** cuts through the air in a loud, clear, and sharp way. *The ring of the phone **pierced** the silence of the room.*

plateau: A piece of high, flat land. *He could look down on the entire city when he climbed up to the **plateau**.*

plea: If you beg someone to do something, you are making a **plea**. *His mother ignored his **plea** for a second piece of cake.*

plotting: To **plot** is to map out or plan something. *The travelers were **plotting** their trip on the road map.*

prance: To **prance** is to walk in a lively, proud way. *My sister likes to **prance** around the room, pretending she is in a fashion show.*

precautions: If you take **precautions**, you do things to make sure something bad doesn't happen later. *Hockey players take **precautions** like wearing helmets and knee pads so they don't get hurt during a game.*

pried: To **pry** something is to move, raise, or pull it apart with force. *We **pried** the rusty nails out of the wood with a hammer.*

profusely: When you do something **profusely**, you do it many times—maybe even more than enough. *I apologized **profusely** for hitting my friend with the ball while we were playing catch.*

promptly: When something is done **promptly**, it is done right away or exactly at a certain time. *We went **promptly** to the theater when we found out the movie was starting in fifteen minutes. After the bell rings, every student **promptly** starts the morning work.*

qualities: Character traits. *His best **qualities** are his honesty and his kindness.*

quench: To **quench** something is to put an end to it or to satisfy it. *You might **quench** your thirst with a large glass of water.*

quiver: A carrier for arrows.

raid: To **raid** a place is to attack it suddenly and by surprise, often to steal from it. *The soldiers were afraid that the enemy army might **raid** their camp.* A **raid** is a surprise attack. *They planned a **raid** of the enemy's storehouses to take all of their food.*

rapped: To **rap** is to knock sharply several times in a row. *When the doorbell didn't work, she **rapped** against the wooden door instead.*

reassuring: When you are nervous or worried, something **reassuring** makes you feel better and comforts you. *My piano teacher's **reassuring** words help me stay calm before a performance.*

recited: To **recite** is to say or repeat something out loud, usually something you have learned by heart. *He stood in front of the class and **recited** the poem he had memorized.*

reduced: To **reduce** something is to make it smaller. *The baseball team was **reduced** to eight members when the shortstop moved away.*

reflecting: When something is **reflecting** on a shiny surface, it is showing back a picture of itself, like a mirror does. *The window glass is **reflecting** my face, showing me my smile.*

relief: Help for people who are in trouble. *The workers provided **relief** to the town that was hit by a hurricane, bringing supplies and medicine with them.* **Relief** can also mean feeling better after you've been bothered by something for a long time. *He felt a huge sense of **relief** once the test was over.*

reluctantly: If you do something **reluctantly**, you do it even though you don't really want to. *If you are having fun at a party, you are probably going to leave **reluctantly**.*

reservoir: A large lake, either natural or made by people, that is used to store a city's or town's water.

rigid: Something **rigid** is stiff and unmoving. *When my sister broke her leg, the doctor put it in a **rigid** cast.*

rosin: A sticky material rubbed on the bows of string instruments, like violins or cellos, to help the bows slide better against the strings.

rubble: The broken pieces left over when something is destroyed or crumbled. *The earthquake turned the building into a pile of **rubble**.*

rudder: A **rudder** is the long, flat piece of metal or wood attached to the back of a boat that sailors use to steer.

sacred: Something **sacred** is holy according to a person's religion. *In India, people who practice the Hindu religion consider cows **sacred** and will not eat them.*

scarce: When something is **scarce**, it is rare or hard to find, or there is not enough of it. *Plants and animals are **scarce** in the desert because there is so little water.*

scroll: Rolls of paper or parchment (specially prepared animal skin) that can be written on.

scrub: Short, skinny bushes or trees. ***Scrub** is not very strong or tall and it is easier to pull out than fully grown trees or bushes.*

scurried: To **scurry** is to move quickly with short, fast steps. *When we saw the bus coming, we **scurried** outside so we wouldn't miss it.*

sensation: A **sensation** is a feeling in your body or a part of your body. *The mosquito bites on her leg gave her a burning, itching **sensation**.* A **sensation** can also be a general feeling that something is happening. *He had the strange **sensation** that he was floating in mid-air.*

shell: A type of bomb that is shot from a cannon or a large gun.

signified: Showed. *Her framed award **signified** that she hadn't missed a single day of school.*

slunk: Moved in a quiet, sneaky way. **Slunk** is the past tense of *slink. The cat **slunk** through the grass, trying to catch a mouse.*

smug: When you are **smug**, you show satisfaction or pride about something in a way that's likely to annoy other people. *The girl who won the race was so **smug** that she talked about her trophy all day.*

snickers: A **snicker** is a quiet and nasty laugh. *When the actor tripped onstage, **snickers** filled the theater.*

soothed: To **soothe** is to help someone relax or to feel less pain. *When the baby cries, he can be **soothed** if you rock him gently.*

spellbound: When you are **spellbound**, you are so interested in what you are seeing or hearing that you don't pay attention to anything else. *The movie was so exciting and unusual that it had them **spellbound**.*

splintered: Something **splintered** is broken into many small and sharp pieces. *After the baseball hit the window, there was **splintered** glass all over the ground.*

staked out: To **stake out** a piece of land is to plant wooden or metal posts in the ground to show that you claim it. *The campers **staked out** their campsite to keep other people from taking it.*

strained: To **strain** is to struggle to do something. *The worker **strained** to lift the heavy barrels into the truck.*

stubs: The **stub** of a pencil or crayon is the short part left over after you've used most of it up. *All my favorite colored pencils have been worn down to **stubs** because I draw with them so much.*

sufficient: Enough, or as much as someone would need or want. *I'm not very hungry, so half a sandwich will be **sufficient** for my lunch.*

surging: Something that is **surging** is moving strongly in a certain direction, like a wave. *As soon as the doors opened, the crowd began **surging** into the theater.*

suspicions: When you have **suspicions**, you have a strong feeling about something (especially something wrong or bad) but you don't know for certain. *I had **suspicions** that the man had stolen something when I saw him run quickly out of the store.*

tan: To **tan** an animal skin means to make it into leather.

tantalizing: Something is **tantalizing** if you want it very badly but you cannot have it right away. *A piece of chocolate cake is **tantalizing** if you know you have to finish your dinner before you can eat it.*

throbbed: If a part of your body **throbs**, you feel fast, regular waves of pain. *Her stubbed toe **throbbed** with pain for hours.*

thyme: A strong-smelling plant with small leaves that are used in cooking.

till: When you **till** a piece of land, you prepare it for growing crops. *A farmer will **till** the soil with a plow to make it easier to plant seeds.*

torment: To **torment** is to cause great pain, suffering, or worry. *Your father might tell you not to **torment** your sister if you were pulling her hair or teasing her.*

tracer: A type of bullet that leaves a trail of light behind it when it flies through the air.

trappings: In this story, **trappings** are a fancy harness or covering for a horse or other riding animal.

troubleshooters: People whose job it is to fix problems.

turn the other cheek: If someone tells you to "**turn the other cheek**," they are telling you not to fight back when someone hurts you with words or actions.

vibrated: To **vibrate** is to move back and forth very quickly. *The phone **vibrated** on the table, making a buzzing noise.*

virtue: When you behave with **virtue**, it means you know and do what is right. *When you are honest, kind, or helpful, you are showing **virtue**.*

wheezed: To **wheeze** is to breathe loudly and painfully, or to make a noise that sounds like that kind of breathing—a scratchy or whistling noise. *You might **wheeze** if you are allergic to something like pollen or dust. The engine **wheezed** a few times before the car ran out of gas.*

Winsor Dam and Goodnough Dike: The two large dams that hold in the water of the Quabbin Reservoir.

wistfully: If you do something **wistfully**, you do it sadly, as if you wish you could be doing something else. *The dog looked out the window **wistfully** as the family left the house without him.*

witnessed: To **witness** something is to see it happen. *We **witnessed** the fireworks because we happened to be nearby when they started.*

woodpeckers: A term for the men hired to cut down trees for the Quabbin Reservoir, used to show that many of them did not have a lot of experience with the job.

worrywart: A **worrywart** is someone who worries a lot without a good reason. *Someone might say you are a **worrywart** if you are concerned there won't be enough food at your birthday party even though you bought two cakes.*

ACKNOWLEDGMENTS

All possible care has been taken to trace ownership and secure permission for each selection in this series. The Great Books Foundation wishes to thank the following authors, publishers, and representatives for permission to reproduce copyrighted material:

Tuesday of the Other June, by Norma Fox Mazer, from SHORT TAKES: A SHORT STORY COLLECTION FOR YOUNG READERS, edited by Elizabeth Segel. Copyright © 1986. Reproduced by permission of Elaine Markson Literary Agency.

DOESN'T FALL OFF HIS HORSE, by Virginia A. Stroud. Copyright © 1994, 2010 by Virginia A. Stroud. Reproduced by permission of Dwyer and O'Grady, Inc.

THE CELLO OF MR. O, by Jane Cutler. Copyright © 1999 by Jane Cutler. Reproduced by permission of SLL/Sterling Lord Literistic, Inc.

The No-Guitar Blues, from BASEBALL IN APRIL AND OTHER STORIES, by Gary Soto. Copyright © 1990 by Gary Soto. Reproduced by permission of Houghton Mifflin Harcourt Publishing Company.

The Fire on the Mountain, from THE FIRE ON THE MOUNTAIN AND OTHER STORIES FROM ETHIOPIA AND ERITREA, by Harold Courlander and Wolf Leslau. Copyright © 1978 by Harold Courlander and Wolf Leslau. Reproduced by permission of the Emma Courlander Trust.

Ooka and the Honest Thief, from OOKA THE WISE: TALES OF OLD JAPAN, by I. G. Edmonds. Copyright © 1961, 1989 by I. G. Edmonds. Reproduced by permission of Barry Malzberg.

THE OLD WOMAN AND THE WAVE, by Shelley Jackson. Copyright © 1998 by Shelley Jackson. Reproduced by permission of Shelley Jackson and BookStop Literary Agency, LLC.

LETTING SWIFT RIVER GO, by Jane Yolen. Copyright © 1992 by Jane Yolen. Print edition reproduced by permission of Little, Brown and Company. Audio and ebook editions reproduced by permission of Curtis Brown, Ltd.

THE APPLE AND THE ENVELOPE, by Herbert Montgomery. Copyright © 1973 by Holt, Rinehart, and Winston, Inc. Reproduced by permission of Ann M. Riley.

ILLUSTRATION CREDITS

Illustrations for *Tuesday of the Other June* copyright © 2014 by Terry Julien.

Illustrations for *Doesn't Fall Off His Horse* copyright © 1994, 2010 by Virginia A. Stroud. Reproduced by permission of Dwyer and O'Grady, Inc.

Illustrations for *The Cello of Mr. O* copyright © 1999 by Greg Couch. Reproduced by permission of Dutton Children's Books, a division of Penguin Group (USA) LLC.

Illustrations for *The No-Guitar Blues* copyright © 2014 by Rich Lo.

Illustrations for *The Fire on the Mountain* and *Ooka and the Honest Thief* copyright © 1992 by Leo and Diane Dillon.

Illustrations for *The Old Woman and the Wave* copyright © 1998 by Shelley Jackson. Reproduced by permission of Shelley Jackson and BookStop Literary Agency, LLC.

Illustrations for *Letting Swift River Go* copyright © 2011 by Rich Lo.

Illustrations for *The Apple and the Envelope* copyright © 2014 by Adam Gustavson.

Cover art copyright © 2014 by Helen Cann.

Design by THINK Book Works.